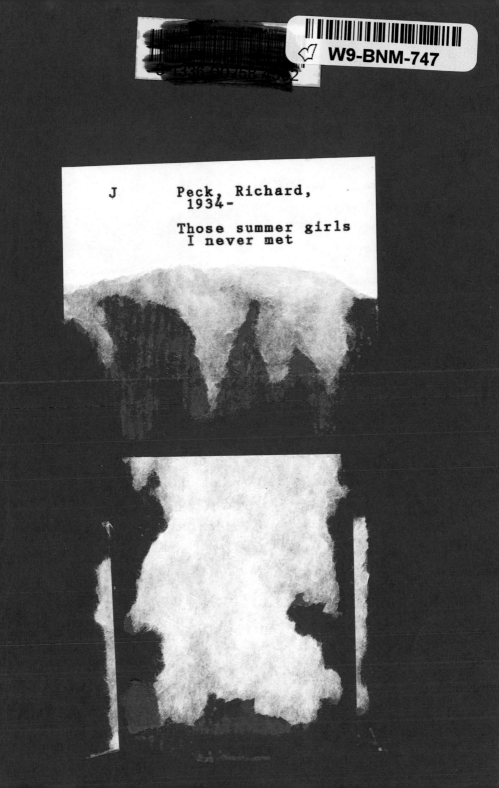

Those Summer Girls I Never Met

Also by Richard Peck

NOVELS FOR YOUNG PEOPLE
Don't Look and It Won't Hurt
Dreamland Lake
Through a Brief Darkness
Representing Super Doll
The Ghost Belonged to Me
Ghosts I Have Been
Are You in the House Alone?
Father Figure
Secrets of the Shopping Mall
Close Enough to Touch
The Dreadful Future of Blossom Culp
Remembering the Good Times
Blossom Culp and the Sleep of Death
Princess Ashley

NOVELS FOR ADULTS
Amanda/Miranda
New York Time
This Family of Women

PICTURE BOOKS
Monster Night at Grandma's House
(ILLUSTRATED BY DON FREEMAN)

NONFICTION ANTHOLOGIES
Edge of Awareness
(Coedited with Ned E. Hoopes)
Leap into Reality

VERSE ANTHOLOGIES
Sounds and Silences
Mindscapes
Pictures That Storm Inside My Head

Those Summer Girls I Never Met

RICHARD PECK

Delacorte Press

Published by
Delacorte Press
The Bantam Doubleday Dell Publishing Group, Inc.
666 Fifth Avenue
New York, New York 10103

LIBRARY OF CONGRESS CATALOGING IN PUBLICATION DATA

Peck, Richard 1934–
    Those summer girls I never met/Richard Peck
      p.   cm.
    Summary: Drew and Steph, ages almost-sixteen and fourteen, reluctantly take a Baltic cruise with their heretofore unknown grandmother, a singing star of the 1940s, and have the experience of a lifetime.
      ISBN 0–440–50054–0
      [1. Grandmothers—Fiction. 2. Cruise ships—Fiction.
3. Brothers and sisters—Fiction.]   I. Title.
PZ7.P338Tf 1988
[Fic]—dc19   88–414
                         CIP
                         AC

Manufactured in the United States of America

September 1988

10 9 8 7 6 5 4 3 2 1

BG

to Jack Cook, voyager

Those Summer Girls I Never Met

Chapter 1

Last day of tenth grade, and I'm through at noon. The English final was a shoo-in, because I'm pretty verbal except around girls. And I survived History. In fact, sophomore year is history. When we stroll back in school next fall, we'll be juniors. We won't even stroll. We'll drive.

I put the finals-week smell behind me: sweat and Xeroxes. Anxiety. Standing out on the school steps, I raise hairless arms to the sun in thanksgiving. It's a golden day, and the world's in bloom. I take an hour walking home past lawns with grass like Easter baskets. I'm taking my time because it's the kind of day you'd like to be twenty-two years old with nobody on your case and a line of established credit.

Anyway, Bates Morthland has his bio final this afternoon before we can get together for one of our

1

planning sessions. Bates and I have the same June birthday, proof right there that we're friends for the long haul. So we've got to get our heads together and refine a few summer plans. Driver's licenses. Jobs if we can find something after our birthdays. And girls. Maybe even girls.

Right now I don't know any girls, not well, not even freshmen. But Bates and I have this theory: that once we've got those driver's licenses in our pockets, we'll have an edge. We're going to have something to say to girls. We'll even know girls to say something to. Bates and I don't know how we know these things. We just know these things.

We know timing is everything, and cool counts. Bates was born cool, but he's had to get through ninth and tenth grade like anybody else.

"This is the summer we're going to come into our own," he says.

Today's the first time since Christmas I haven't walked out of school with a book in my hand. Occasionally homework, but mostly a well-thumbed copy of Ivan Lendl's *Hitting Hot,* so I can read up on ground strokes, lobs, serves, volleys. I don't play tennis, but in tenth grade you need your props. I don't play basketball, either, but, hey, if I grow another foot and a half during the next two years and develop a hook shot, I could have major universities looking at me.

At twelve thirty-five by my Swatch, I'm at the corner of Hickory and Fielding Drive, and a shadow's falling across my noon. The truth is, the summer I've been playing in my head isn't going to happen, not the way Bates and I have it laid out.

He doesn't know it yet, but I've been stringing us both along since April because I'm not even going to be here for the first two weeks, including our mutual birthday. We've been working out this summer, minute by minute, and I'm not even going to be here for the first, crucial part. I haven't gotten around to mentioning this to Bates, not with the kind of plans we've been working up.

We were going to be down at Motor Vehicles at dawn on our birthday. Except it's not going to happen that way. By the time I get back here, I could be a total stranger to everybody—to Bates, and to all those summer girls I never met.

Why haven't I been straight with my best friend about this? Well, let's see. I'm a procrastinator, though I've been trying to get over it. And frankly, I thought I could talk my mom out of the whole deal. As a rule, she isn't this hard to handle. Besides, until the day school's out, summer always looks out of reach. It's way out there on the horizon, except that now I'm looking summer in the face. And I don't like what I see.

I'm walking as slow as I can without losing ground, but my house is starting to loom up.

Mom's Hyundai is parked in the drive, winking in

the sun. But why? She's a legal secretary, very programed, and she doesn't come home for lunch, and this isn't a national holiday. Then I hear my sister's voice.

The whole neighborhood's hearing it. It's Stephanie-the-bullhorn, and it's polluting whole subdivisions. You can't hear what she's screaming. From here it's just raw, fourteen-year-old rage. There are gaps between howls, as Mom tries to get in some quick, low-pitched words.

I stroll to a stop and hear Steph bang the door of her room upstairs. A soft implosion from this distance, but it sends out shock waves. Hedges quiver.

Steph is all-suburban champion door-banger for her weight and class. She practices. One time I caught her out in the hall banging the door, and she wasn't even going into her room. She's in there a lot, though, with her Walkman in one ear and her Trimline in the other and a VCR running. She mainly yells and maybe to hear herself.

She just turned fourteen, but she says she's as good as sixteen, practically seventeen. I'll actually be sixteen in a couple of weeks.

"So what does this mean?" I asked her once. "Do you think of me as your younger brother?"

"I don't think of you at all," Steph said, "and keep out of my room, right?"

"Forbidden City," I said, and she seemed to grasp it. I have no reason to go in her room. It's a mess because she knows it annoys Mom. My room's a mess, too, but only because it's how I can find my stuff.

I ease into the back door and find the kitchen empty. The floor tile's winking like the Hyundai, and not a crumb on the toaster. Mom leaves it that way every morning. When she comes home at night, she tries to make up for having a job all day. She fixes whole meals from scratch and starts baking. The fact that she kind of excuses herself for supporting us hasn't quite dawned on me yet.

I see a couple more minutes of unstructured time if I can get up to my room. Starting up the stairs, I don't look into the living room. The upstairs hall is carpeted, but evidently Steph isn't back into her Walkman yet. She's heard me and thinks it's Mom.

"I'm not going and that's final!" she screams through her door. "Is that clear?"

She can make herself clear through steel plates. She opens the door, sees me there, and bangs it again. My head rings. I've given her this extra opportunity, and she's gotten a bang out of it.

I lope on down to my room, littered with study notes for exams. Now they're ancient relics, like cub scout badges. I'm hardly ever in this room during the day. Even the light looks funny. My closet door's open because it's never been closed. An alien object's swaying from the closet pole. From here I see a shoulder, an arm: chalky white. Tags are hanging down from it.

5

It's a new white dinner jacket, double breasted, and black tux pants with a shiny stripe. It's one hot rig, but what am I doing with it? The senior prom is still two years from tonight, and I probably won't be going because I don't know any girls. And I'm not getting married, for the same reason.

I turn to my bed. If I got sick, I could stay up here and then recover in time for the driver's license exam. Sudden inspirations like this one have kept me from telling my news to Bates. Even now I still think a foolproof plan will drop in my lap. I've heard of this disease called cat-scratch fever, which mimics mononucleosis. But you only get cat-scratch fever from cats, and you only get mono from kissing. This leaves me out twice. Still, I check out the bed and hear Mom's voice.

"Drew?"

It's coming from somewhere in the house, a voice like velvet, after Steph's.

"Drew?"

As I walk past Steph's door for the second time, it's opening. Steph shows me an eye: purple eye paint shading to yellow. I happen to know where she got that: off a music video of Cyndi Lauper's.

"Listen," Steph hisses.

I see half of her mouth: no paint, like a little girl. Maybe she's screamed off her lip gloss. "Don't let her talk you into *anything*, right? You know how she is. She never listens. She never thinks about me. But don't give in, okay? This is serious. It's life threatening. You two better not gang up on me, right?"

"Right," I say. She can gang up on us all by herself, but it's not supposed to work the other way. "Stay cool," I tell her, but she's not into irony.

Mom's in the living room, posed. She's still in her skirt from work, and her feet are close together under the coffee table. She's on the sofa in front of Grandmother's picture. We don't even use the living room much anymore. And Grandmother's picture? I haven't seen it in years.

I don't ask Mom why she's taking a half day off from work when she never does. I know. We're getting down to the wire now, and counting in hours. My summer fantasies are in deadly peril.

Slipping out of her shoes, she tucks her legs up under her. She's going casual on me. You have to watch her or she'll do that. She's always pulled together for work, but around the house she kicks back, in Levi's and no makeup to speak of. Her shoes are flat heeled because she's always thought she was too tall. It took me till fifteen to be as tall as she is. Then I shot up a couple more inches, for emphasis. I'm not sure what she looks like. She's always been here.

And I can't sit here and sulk. I'm practically a junior.

"Bad scene with Steph," I say.

She brushes back her hair with a hand, still casual

. . . too casual, like it hasn't hurt her. It always hurts. She always loses.

"I keep thinking," she says, "that if I'm this positive . . . low-key role model, sooner or later Steph will see that, and want to be that."

She's wrong, of course. Dead wrong. Steph isn't going to want to be Mom. Mom never wins, so Steph thinks she's a wimp.

And Mom doesn't want to put me on the spot. I'm not exactly the man of the family because I'm not exactly a man yet. Mom tries to remember that, but now she really wants me on her side.

What do I want? I want Bates Morthland to get his tail over here so we can make some major summer plans, starting *now.*

"Drew, you've got to back me up with Stephanie."

So we're into it.

"Mom, do you know what Steph's worst nightmare is? It's that she'd have to spend her summer—"

"Not the whole summer."

"Mom, please. Hear me out. Her worst nightmare would be to have to spend it with me. Her geeky big brother." I jerk a thumb at myself. "And worse. She'd have to spend it with me in foreign countries, even on a boat where there's no escape. And here's Ground Zero, Mom. She'd be off her turf, away from her little nerdlet friends. She couldn't call anybody up. I don't know, maybe she couldn't even pick up anything on her Walkman. Mom, we're talking

Steph's worst Stephen King nightmare. It's worse than—"

I was about to say it's worse than when Dad cut out. But we don't deal with that, and he's been gone quite a while. I was just going into middle school, and Steph was in the grades, but we don't deal with it. Mom smoothed it over so much that for a long time I expected him back. He's not coming back. He's married again, in Colorado.

The checks come regularly. The letters come once in a while. I send him a school picture. He fires back a good reason for not getting back to see us. I used to invite myself out to see him in the summers, but he always had a conflict. Now I don't even want to be away from home in the summer, or have I already mentioned that?

Mom doesn't deal with any of it. She married for life. I don't know what she calls what's happening to her now. That's why we hardly ever use this living room. It's for a whole family. It's probably full of stuff they got for wedding presents. But we're here now, maybe because Mom's lost too many battles with Steph in the kitchen.

"I try to take it easy with her," Mom says. "Fourteen's a hard age, for one thing."

For another thing, she goes easy on both of us to make up for Dad, and Steph really uses that. I probably do, too, but try not to. I'm trying not to now.

Steph's about to convince herself that Mom wants

9

to get rid of us. "She's probably going to have an *affair* or something this summer," Steph says.

"I don't even want you both to be away this summer," Mom's saying to me, "or even part of the summer."

"Well, then—"

"But this is important, Drew. Your grandmother really wants you and Stephanie with her. She doesn't ask for much, you know. She's . . . very independent. She wants to get to know you both, before you're grown up."

My elbows are on my knees, and I'm talking into my fists, and I'm not being a day older than I am.

"Then why doesn't she come for a visit—here?"

Mom sighs. "Do you realize what this trip would cost if we had to pay for it? She's trying to give you both a wonderful experience."

Mom's on shaky ground now. What's so wonderful about a wonderful experience if nobody wants it? She just stopped herself from mentioning all those kids who'd jump at a chance like this. Because there aren't that many. At our age, if there's one thing you don't want to see, it's the world.

"Why are you fighting this, Drew? You've known since April."

This I can't deny. In April Mom got Steph and me in the Hyundai and drove us to this place in the mall where they take little pictures of you. I look about twelve in my picture. Steph's so mad she looks like an ax murderess, which is actually a pretty good likeness.

Then we sent these pictures to an office and got back regulation U.S. passports. For days I pretended mine was a driver's license. Why not? It's an official document; it's got my picture on it and my name: Andrew W. Wingate; and it'll take me places. But it's a passport.

This looks like one time Mom isn't caving in. For some reason she's gone hardliner on us. It looks a lot like we're going to take our passports and go see Grannie, who's this person we don't really know.

"She's this person we don't really know."

"You know her," Mom says, weary. "She was here —how long ago was it?"

"See? We can't remember."

"You were about fifth grade." Mom waits for me to remember, but I hold off. "Can't you think of something else that happened around then?"

Yes, Dad left around then, but we haven't ever—

"When your father left, I called Mother. I didn't mean to, but I didn't have anywhere else to turn. She came up from Florida. It wasn't very successful. It wasn't as if she hadn't been divorced herself. She had.

"She didn't particularly like seeing me suffer, but she didn't know what to do about it. All her solutions have always been for herself. And we'd never built anything together. When she left, I was more lost than ever."

I haven't heard Mom talk like this before. I skim over the part about how she and Grandmother had never built anything together. I haven't given much thought to the connections between adults. But I remember now when Grandmother came. The two of them, one tall, the other short and feisty, spent a lot of the time talking loud behind closed doors. I remember Grandmother didn't stay long.

So they never had much of a relationship. I knew that anyway, I guess. And Grandmother doesn't seem to be the type to keep in touch. I've never felt deprived. This is the suburbs, and we aren't much into grandparents around here. Even Bates Morthland, who has everything, only has one grandmother, and she's way off in Laguna Hills, California.

I know he has this grandmother because for years when he was a kid, she'd send him birthday cards addressed to

MASTER BATES MORTHLAND

and nobody in his family could think of a way to stop her.

Anyway, enough about the Morthlands. They don't have problems like this. "So Grandmother let you down about Dad," I say, "so why should she start up now, with Steph and me?"

Mom almost smiles. "Maybe she's mellowing. And

maybe she just feels like having you with her. She likes having her own way. And maybe you'll be glad one day."

It's Mom's concluding argument, but nowhere near her best. Because I figure that one day if I look back on my sixteenth summer and I wasn't right here bagging babes with Bates and reporting to Motor Vehicles at sunrise on our birthday—then I'll know this particular summer was where the rest of my life went wrong. This goes double for Steph, who wasn't planning to do anything for three months but go to the mall.

The front doorbell rings, and it'll be Bates, too late. I'm a dead man and know it. But I'm still fifteen, so I'm out of the chair, half hoping he has a magic cure, a silver bullet—something.

"Bates, my man," I say at the door: hollow voiced, broken.

"Bummer bio," he says in the shorthand we use, especially around adults. Over my shoulder he sees Mom in the living room. And over her shoulder he sees the picture of my grandmother, who also happens to be looking over *her* shoulder.

In a few manly strides he's in the living room, sure as always of his welcome. Mom's smiling up at him, but he's looking past her at the picture.

He points right at Grannie and says, "Okay, what's the joke?"

Bates and I are terminally tight. We'd go through fire for each other. But you have to watch him. He runs to extremes. Here lately, he's been getting overly preppie. His button-down striped dress-shirt's flapping loose over his rear under an upscale Windbreaker. His pleated pants are suitably short in the leg, and his L. L. Bean bluchers are planted firmly in the carpet.

Without my steadying influence, he could go completely mush-mouthed, unbearable preppie this summer. He's right on the cusp now. I could come back and find him wrapped like a mummy in long-tailed wool scarves in the Princeton colors.

There's trouble of this sort in his ancestry. His dad went to the Wharton School of Business, and his mom ran Junior League until they booted her out for turning forty. They have a computer terminal in their bedroom. Things like this get into the genes and can crop up in your offspring. There are some evil omens in the Morthland history.

Also, preppies aren't too subtle.

"No, really," Bates is saying, pointing at Grandmother's picture, "what's the punch line here? What's Connie Carlson doing in your living room?"

He does a heavy buck-and-wing shuffle in his L. L. Beans and hums a few bars of an old song sensation he has no reason even to know. It appears to be "Swingtime Down in Dixie." Bates is a bit of a nostalgia freak. Maybe all preppies are. But I didn't think he went back farther than Chubby Checker. I know he can do all of "Let's Twist Again (Like We Did Last Summer)."

Mom's shrinking slightly. Grandmother's picture isn't out for display. It's out to remind Steph and me of our roots. But now Mom's little plan has gone public. I try to turn Bates by the shoulder, but he's still wingin' and swingin'.

"Bates, let's go for a walk." He keeps on. "Walkies, Bates."

"But first," he says, "what's the Sweetheart of Swingtime doing behind your sofa?"

"It's a long story."

"Look, we've got all summer."

"No, we don't. I don't."

What little color he has drains from his face. He darts a look at Mom. Usually in these cases, it's the parent who's the felon. She's gazing at the carpet. She and Bates have a great rapport, but today nothing's working.

Since we have some topics to cover, I get him to the door. Then I happen to glance back. It's funny how you really see people sometimes when you're just about to leave them. I didn't have that chance with Dad. I didn't know he was going until he was gone.

Mom's still tucked up at the end of the sofa. Maybe I catch a glimpse of her aloneness. Maybe I realize

15

that in the endless weeks ahead, she's going to be alonest of all.

Grandmother's giving me the eye from across the room. Her picture's vintage 1944 stuff, a tricky black-and-white, high-gloss publicity shot. Grannie's smiling over a bare shoulder, sweet and sexy. Her breasts are bursting out of her dress. She's the Queen of Cleavage. Her lacquered black hair is tied up in a big bow. Each one of her eyelashes is featured separately, curving back to her high, arching, painted-on brows. Her mouth's a black cupid's bow. She's blowing kisses to draftees. She's a star of the 1940s.

"She's dead, right?" Bates says in my ear. "Connie Carlson?"

"No, she's still with us. She's my grandmother."

"Pretty amazing," he says, which is our personal shorthand for: You're So Full of It that It's Coming Out Your Ears.

"My grandmother, Bates," I say in a tone he can't mistake, "and she's sending for me and Steph—you know Steph? Dolores Doorbanger? She's sending for both of us. We're going to take this cruise on a ship with her. For weeks. *Two* weeks. I could show you the tickets. I could show you the passports."

We're outside and halfway down the block, heading for The Rock. Bates strokes his chin. It's beginning to square off. All it needs is something to shave, and it'll be like his dad's. "A yacht?"

I'm tempted. It might help, especially with him, if

16

I hint that the grandmother I've never happened to mention happens to have a yacht at her command. I'm tempted, but I'm also a broken man.

"No, Bates. And the summer you and I were planning isn't even going to get off the pad. I'm going to spend the strategic part of it with two females of my family. One of them has the worst case of puberty ever recorded, and the other one's a broken-down band singer. We're going to be in a tub on the ocean."

"Pretty amazing," Bates says faintly, but he's beginning to believe. "Like what ocean?"

"Try the Baltic Sea."

"Far out," Bates says. He believes.

Chapter 2

We make it to The Rock, and already it feels like evening. Maybe it's just my mood. The Rock's in The Park, which once had a playground but the neighbors complained. Now it's a flat grassy square with houses all the way around it. No doubt the developers would like to get their hands on it. At one end is The Rock, left over from the Ice Age, about the size of four Buicks, grouped. On this particular June afternoon, it's still my idea of geography.

Bates and I hang out here. At one time we did a certain amount of smoking on The Rock, and a lot of talking for many years in all weathers. It's one of those things that never changes or goes away, so it has a soothing effect on us.

But our conversation won't flow. We try all afternoon. I kick The Rock a couple of times, which doesn't do much either way.

We even try neutral subjects, but there aren't any. What's there to say about school when it's over? And the topic of girls is linked up with the summer that's not happening. And what else is there?

"A way out?" I ask Bates. "Think of something. The water's closing over my head."

We've been slumped on The Rock, but now he's pacing. "Cut me some slack, man," he says, which means he needs a minute to think. But then all he comes up with is "The situation will come on line."

When he's really stumped, he resorts to computer talk. We're out of options, but then he checks his watch. "Dad'll be home. If there's a way out of this, he'll know it."

One of Bates's peculiarities is a tight relationship with his dad. I don't know which one of them takes after the other. Bates tries to be the mature one, but they're basically chips off of each other's block.

Actually, Bates's dad isn't a bad guy for an elderly preppie with a reputation for bad jokes. He's been pretty good to me over the years. He'd see to it that we both got to Pop Warner football when we were at the end of that phase and my dad was already gone. Bates and I take the extra long way to his house, and when we get there, both the Morthland Lincolns are in the garage.

It's quite a house. Nobody's ever made an accurate room count. Bates's dad is in the den, out of his three-piece pinstripe and into his Ralph Laurens. He's deep in a big leather chair with nailheads, catching up on his *Wall Street Journals*.

"Ah, Morthland and Wingate," he says when he sees us. He's always seemed to think that Bates and I are a law firm. It's a long-dead joke, but he's hanging in with it. "Your mother's up in her room," he tells Bates, "tapping one of her charities into the computer. Your mother has dispensed a lot of charity in that bedroom, as I have good reason to know."

Mr. Morthland fires these laugh lines at us, and they miss us by a mile every time. When he gets a closer look at us, he puts down his *Wall Street Journal*. "Don't trip over those chins, men. What seems to be the trouble?"

We flop down.

"Give it to me straight." Mr. Morthland leans forward over his stomach and checks us out through his little half-moon glasses. "You both flunked your finals and have to repeat tenth grade, right? No? It wouldn't be world peace, I trust?"

"Dad, please, this is serious. Tell him, Drew."

"You tell him." I'm really down.

"Here it is in a nutshell, Dad." The minute Bates starts to talk, he becomes his dad. Their chins look like bookends. "Drew's grandmother is making him go with her on a cruise ship practically all summer. All the Scandinavian capitals and Russia, plus London. Right, Drew?"

"Ah." Mr. Morthland pulls on his chin. "What's the ship?"

"Dad, what does it *matter?*"

"The *Regal Voyager,*" I mutter.

"Stopover in London before or after the cruise?" Mr. Morthland inquires.

"Before."

"London hotel?"

I reach around in my mind for the name. "The Clarence."

Mr. Morthland surveys his ceiling. "That's about a five-thousand-dollar cruise package to some of the most interesting ports in the world. Top-of-the-line vessel too. I see you've got a serious problem here, Drew."

"Dad, this is no laughing matter." Bates chops the air with a square hand. "We can't just blow this off. Drew and I were planning—"

"Tell me about your grandmother, Drew," Mr. Morthland says.

Hot blood rises up my narrow neck. I hadn't thought this far. Somehow I don't want to tell him about Grandmother. Somehow she doesn't fit in here. I stare down into the priceless Oriental rug.

"She's a singer," helpful Bates says. "At least she used to be. They've invited her on the ship for a couple of cruises to—do a few songs, or whatever. You've heard of her, Dad. She used to be Connie Carlson."

21

Since I'm looking at the rug, I don't actually see Mr. Morthland come out of his chair. *Wall Street Journals* skid across the floor. He's standing over me. I'm looking down at his pair of blue-on-brown L. L. Bean bluchers.

"Drew, does my son speak the truth? Is your grandmother Connie Carlson?"

Now I'm looking Mr. Morthland in the fly. I look all the way up. His half-glasses are on the top of his head now. His hands are on his hips.

"Yeah," I say.

"Cow Cow Boogie," he says.

I blink.

Bearing down on me, he says, "This means nothing to you?"

It could be a song title. I shake my head. He snaps his fingers at Bates.

"Son, go over to the files and get that Dorsey Brothers Orchestra record. It's under D. Snap to."

The old jokey Mr. Morthland seems to have left us. Bates is across the den opening up paneled doors and going through a world-class cassette and record collection.

Mr. Morthland rounds on me again. "It'll be scratchy. It's an old forty-five, and I didn't buy it new, and I've played it nearly bald, all right?"

"All right."

"It's not the real Dorsey sound anyway, but Jimmy kept the band going a while after Tommy died. I've got the definitive lineup on Tommy: 'the Sentimental Gentleman of Swing.' A little before my time, but what the heck. The Pied Pipers? Sinatra? Dick Haymes? Jo Stafford—and fed from behind by Buddy Rich's drums. You want to hear a trumpet solo? Try Max Kaminsky. You want to hear music for the first time in your life? Listen to this."

The den doesn't exactly fill with sound. It's like music coming from another room, a little thin, with a tick every time the needle hits a flaw. Mr. Morthland looks up from the turntable and shrugs. "Nineteen fifty-five," he says.

There's a big buildup from the orchestra, and then somebody's singing: a girl, a woman. "So Rare" is the name of the song, but the words aren't that distinct. It's a voice off a late movie, out of a time capsule: rich, full, and taking its time.

It's my grandmother singing, but that fact doesn't really sink in. I never thought of her cutting records. We don't seem to have any of them. I just thought she sang with a band, or something. I didn't know there was—evidence. I didn't know there were fans.

Mr. Morthland seems to be swaying. Bates is over by the window, looking out, detaching. Possibly he's revising his summer plans.

"By then she had it all. This is the matured voice you're listening to," Mr. Morthland says, maybe because he knows we don't know how to hear her. How could we? What do we have to compare this sound to, Def Leppard?

When it's over, Mr. Morthland lifts the needle, gently. "That one earned them a Gold Disc. But the glory days were about over by then. By the mid-fifties you had your Sauter-Finegan sound moving in. And out on the Coast, Shelley Manne and Shorty Rogers and those fellows were beginning to make changes. But, boy, it was something in its day. It was the last music people really loved."

Bates turns from the window, not so detached. "People love rock, Dad. They love heavy metal."

Mr. Morthland just smiles down at the record. "That noise is for loving yourself. This music's for loving someone else."

This is a new Mr. Morthland to me. He never got this fired up over Pop Warner football. And this is the guy Bates and I thought might save my summer?

"I wish I were going to be in your shoes," he tells me.

I nod. I wish he were too.

It's time to go, but Mr. Morthland's with us all the way to the front door. He keeps thinking of things he wants to tell me.

"Listen, Drew, she was no Helen Forrest, who was really the top. And she wasn't Lee Wiley. She didn't know her way around a ballad like Ginny Simms. But your grandmother was very good at what she did, better than a lot of people knew. It wasn't a big voice, but she had versatility and drive. She had something special. She felt it, so you felt it. Here." He taps his chest.

He's speaking a foreign language, but I'm picking up all I want to.

"And she's been out of the public eye for quite a few years. You can't expect a lot from her now. Tell you what, I'll dig up some more of her work. She did some of the first stereophonics, on the Command label. Then you'll get a better idea."

I nod, but I won't be here. I'm leaving tomorrow, a fact I find hard to put into words. I've told Bates, and that's enough. Mr. Morthland starts to leave us in peace, but pops back.

"Do nothing till you hear from me," he says.

"Okay."

"No, that was one of your grandmother's big songs. I've got it on an old acetate. Ask her to sing it on the ship. She could always stop the show with that one."

"Okay."

We finally get away from him, but we have to go out in the yard to do it.

"So much for interfacing with parental units," Bates says. "What can I say? Maybe you'll be captured by terrorists, get ransomed, and be home ahead of schedule."

"Thanks, that helps."

"You'll be home way before school starts anyway. There'll be a lot of summer left."

"Yeah, you can meet me at the plane. You'll be driving by then," I say, bitter.

"You'll be driving yourself by the next day. What's the difference?"

"*A lot,*" we say in unison.

It gives us the first laugh of the day and probably the last of the summer.

"Well, see you," I say, turning away, moving out.

Behind me, Bates says, "Bon voyage, okay?"

Ice bobs in the water, and wet beads run down my glass. I'm at one end of the dining-room table, and Mom's at the other. Call this the Last Supper.

Upstairs my full suitcase is yawning on the bed, and Mom's given me a new flight bag as a going-away present. Next to my plate are envelopes with tickets and things in them that we'll have to go over. Grandmother's sent the tickets. She's also sent my new dinner jacket. Have I mentioned that it's a gift from her? No, because it's not happening in my head. *She's* not real yet.

The table's set for three, with candles. But Steph naturally isn't here. Her phone rang a while ago, and she needs less excuse than that for missing a meal. Eating with her nearest relatives kills her appetite. Her room smells like a deli, and she does a lot of feeding straight from the refrigerator, off-hours.

Mom's put forth quite a bit of effort and fixed all my favorites, even twice-baked potatoes. But stuff keeps sticking in my throat. I glance down the table, but there are two candle flames between us. I just see the halo of Mom's hair. Seems like I've spent the entire day with adults.

"Mr. Morthland turns out to be a big Connie Carlson fan."

Mom looks up. "Is he? That's . . . good."

"You've never especially wanted anybody to know about her—Grandmother."

Mom wants to protest that. I sense her tensing up. Instead she says, "I never thought people would understand. They've never lived that way. When I was a little girl, I was on the road with Mother most of the time and going to school when I could. I knew that life and nothing else. On the bus, off the bus. Once on the band bus all the way across the country from the Glen Island Casino to Elitch's Gardens in Denver."

This is slightly more than I've ever heard about Mom's childhood. On the other hand, I've never asked.

"A rough life?"

"I didn't think so. I'd wake up in the mornings and see little towns out the bus window, with real houses and kids in the yards. Wash on the line. But no, I didn't mind. I liked the bus, and belonging."

She's quiet a moment and then says, "I don't suppose I did belong, not really. I didn't have any talent. That was pretty clear to both of us. When I was fourteen, Mother sent me to a boarding school. It had to have been a hardship for her, financially. She wouldn't have been getting many bookings by then, but I guess it was worth it to her. She never—I never went back to her. If I couldn't be with her, and like her, I wanted to be like regular people. So I decided to want what the other girls at school wanted. A house. A husband. Children."

Mom stops to think about that. "I never had a father, none I knew. I guess he was a soldier, during the war. Not very important to Mother. I wanted my children to have a father. I tried to be like everybody else. Funny how hard that turned out to be."

She's been talking quietly. Now she stops. Sometimes when you keep your voice low, Steph creeps partway down the stairs to listen, but I don't hear her. Mom and I have finished pretending to eat the meal. Now we're going to pretend to eat dessert.

When she goes to the kitchen for it, she stops and hovers over me while she takes my plate away. "You're not worried, are you? About being in new places? I hadn't thought about that. When I was a kid, we went everywhere."

I realize I'm scared spitless. I've been freaked all along, and fighting it. I'm fifteen and I don't like change. I don't even like TV specials. I like regular programing. I'll be scared of junior year if I live to see it.

So after dessert, we review the envelopes. We've got the plane tickets to London on British Airways.

We've got a couple of thick packets from the Regal Cruise Line. Our tickets, Steph's and mine, luggage tags, traveler's checks, vouchers for the hotel in London, a few brochures showing gray-headed people having a whale of a good time on the good ship *Regal Voyager*. And our passports, of course. There's a packet of British money Mom's picked up at an exchange place.

I dump it out: five-pound notes with the queen of England on them, a confusing mass of coins, with a guide to tell how much they're worth. To keep calm, I mess with the money.

Steph walks in. She's a real vision: torn shirt, baggy camouflage shorts, bare feet. She's been washing her hair, and it's still standing up, half blow-dried with little rivers down her neck. Her face is dead pale, ghostly.

"How about some dessert, honey?" Mom says in the upbeat tone she uses with Steph and never gets back.

"Gillian Bergner called me," she says, trancelike, staring ahead at nothing. It doesn't sound like network news to me. Gillian Bergner calls her four times a night and sits in homeroom with her.

"Gillian's going up to Wisconsin to Conference Point Camp this summer, as a junior counselor."

Mom and I listen. As a rule, Steph isn't into sharing.

She looks at the ceiling, and her eyes brim with tears. "You don't even know what I'm talking about,

29

do you? You never do, do you? Gillian and I had plans for this summer, really important plans. And she just calls up like it's nothing and goes, 'Listen, Stephy, I had this opportunity, and, like, I couldn't pass it up, right? Because at camp there'll be, you know, high-school guys?' And then she goes, 'But it's cool because you're going to Europe or someplace anyway, right?' "

There's a sob in Steph's throat, but she gets through to her big finish. "Then Gillian just goes, 'See you next fall,' and hangs up."

Not quite. They were on the phone forty-five minutes, minimum, but we get the picture. Steph's life is over. She drops down into a chair and slumps. It happens to be at the place set for her. We're all three at the same table. It's a mob scene.

She's about resigned to going to Europe or someplace with her geeky big brother. She's a broken woman, but it took the mighty Gillian Bergner to bring her down. Steph stares into a candle flame, thinking seriously of having hysterics.

Then she realizes she's at the table with us, and leaps up. She's about to make one of her exits, but I've annoyed her by going back to my new coin collection.

"What's that supposed to be?" she says.

"British money. We'll need it in London."

She looks closer at it through narrow eyes.

"I'm not going to use that stuff. It's not real. I'll use real money."

Then she sort of sleepwalks out of the room. After a minute, we hear her door bang.

Mom starts clearing the table.

"I'm not sure I can handle her," I say.

"Just get her there," Mom says. "Your grandmother will do the rest."

It's a thought. "But you said you went away to school when you were Steph's age. Grandmother won't have any experience, especially with somebody like Steph."

I happen to notice Mom's smiling. "Serve her right," she murmurs. "Serve them both right." Then she moves off to the kitchen with a little spring in her step.

31

Chapter 3

~~~~~~~~~~~~~~~~~~~~~~~~~~~~~~~~~~~~~~~

For the next day, maybe two, we're all over the map and going through time zones. Mom sees us off at O'Hare Airport, and I'm wearing my Timberland boots and everything else I couldn't pack. The dinner jacket took up a lot of the suitcase, and Mom bought me black shoes to wear with it. Real shoes. We've gotten Steph this far, but she won't sit with us in the departure lounge.

They're calling our flight to New York, the first lap. When Mom walks me to the end of the passenger line, I decide I better joke it up a little. I smack my forehead.

"I just remembered. I can't go. Who'll do the yard work?" I make a small attempt to escape, but the line's moving. "I wish you were coming with us," I say to Mom. I hadn't thought of it before, but I wish it.

She gives me a smile, a hug. "I wasn't asked," she says.

Steph's somewhere ahead of me. Mom starts up the line to her. Then she stops and gives a private shrug. We passengers file past her into the little tunnel that leads to the big plane.

At JFK Airport in New York I do pretty well getting us from one terminal to the other. Steph isn't clinging to me yet, but she's not keeping her usual distance. Then we're on another plane, this one a wide-body. We have dinner over Nova Scotia, and Steph's in the seat next to me because she got assigned to it.

We've seen the movie before, so she goes to sleep as soon as they dim the lights. She's wearing a pink warm-up jacket and her sixty-dollar running shoes. Also some bad barrettes in her hair. In the middle of the night, she shifts around, and her head's on my shoulder. She drools down my Windbreaker.

I decide I can't sleep sitting up. When I come to, it's broad daylight. My watch says it's two-thirty A.M. None of this makes any sense. I set my watch ahead another five hours. Our fellow passengers are stumbling back to the rest rooms, and coffee's brewing. If I weren't so dog tired, I'd be seriously disoriented. Steph wakes up and looks around through crusty eyes. Without her eye makeup, she looks like a mole.

"You better go to the washroom, and . . . fix yourself," I tell her. "We'll be on the ground pretty soon."

She doesn't bother to answer. She doesn't know anybody in London anyway. She just looks around in her lap, possibly for her phone.

We break through the clouds, and there's land down there. Morning sun glints through the haze off the windshields of toy cars. When we get lower, you can see they're all driving on the wrong side of the roads. Middle Earth.

At Heathrow Airport we get through customs. Suddenly we're out in the main terminal and, I admit, lost, when this beautiful young woman comes up to us.

Whatever she wants, I'm agreeable. It seems she's with Regal Cruise Lines, an escort, and she's spotted us by our luggage tags. When she starts talking about Miss Carlson, it occurs to me she means Grandmother. She's sent word that she'll meet us aboard ship tomorrow when we sail. Miss Carlson's already on the ship, and it hasn't docked yet from the last cruise. I absorb some of this data, but I don't process it.

We're put on a bus with a lot of gray-headed people who have our kind of luggage tags. And finally we're at the Clarence Hotel, which is pretty intimidating. There's a formal dining room off the lobby, full of elderly folks having breakfast.

"I'm not eating in there," Steph says.

A bellhop takes us and our luggage upstairs. Figuring I better tip him, I give him a five-pound note.

"Try again, cock," he says, which really confuses me. I hold out the coins. He takes one and gives me back my fiver.

Fortunately we have separate rooms with a door between that Steph can bang. Once the bellhop leaves, though, she's hanging around in my space. We're even looking out the same window. Being this close to Steph is culture shock all by itself. Besides, I'm in Jetlag Land. I have a short, standing-up dream of Steph and me growing together like Siamese twins. The horror of it clears my head.

Out the window it's a postcard view. Big double-decker red buses and black taxicabs. Domes and towers in the distance. Gold gates at the end of the street into a park. It's Europe or someplace.

"I'm not going out there," Steph whispers. "No way."

Anyhow, we need naps. I notice that when Steph goes into her room, she leaves the door open a wide crack. It's the last thing I notice.

I budget for an hour and a half of concentrated sleep, and this is plenty of time for a nightmare, because I have one. I'm on a big ship with a black-and-white grandmother and Steph in her pink warm-up jacket. The name of the ship is the *Regal Titanic.* Is that an iceberg dead ahead? They're dragging me into a lifeboat, Steph is.

I wake up, and it's Steph, looking strange and damp, pulling on my leg.

"Get up, you *creep,*" she's saying. "Come on. We've got to get out of here. Move your—"

"All right, all right." But where are we? I check my Swatch to see I've been unconscious for six hours. The sun's over on the wrong side of the hotel. And Steph's just about jumping up and down for some reason.

"If you don't get out of that bed, I'm leaving without you," she says, which I doubt.

She gets me out of the room, and I even remember to bring the key. It's pitch black in the hallway. We can't find the elevator, which doesn't matter because it isn't working. We seem to be experiencing a power outage. We feel our way down five flights. The lobby's dim because the power's out down here too. They're beginning to light candles. When we get out onto the bright street, Steph whimpers. But she's dragging me along like she can't wait to see London. She's also peering over her shoulder.

"What's happening, Steph?"

"Nothing. Shut up."

"Steph, we're running for our lives. Why?"

When we get to a corner, she steps in front of a bus barreling along from the wrong direction. I obey my better instincts and drag her back. I don't get thanked for this, but she sees down a side street and heaves up a big sigh.

"Thank heaven. We can eat," she says.

We're within range of one of the better-known

hamburger franchises. A couple of golden mini-arches are laminated onto a three-hundred-year-old wall. Not only is Steph acting weird, she looks weird. It's something about her hair. It's slick down one side. Another of her failed experiments?

Past the golden arches, we're back in friendly territory. We load up, and here they're glad to take my five-pound note. We're into our second sack of fries when I say, "Okay, let's have it. What happened back at the hotel?"

"It wasn't my fault."

"Nothing ever is, Steph. But what happened?"

"It was probably just a coincidence." She even gives herself fangs with a couple of fries, trying to distract me.

"Oh, well, all right," she says. "When I woke up, I had to wash my hair. Then I plugged my hair dryer in, and the light went out."

The light? She shorted out the entire electrical system of a ten-story hotel. But this is still closer to confession than she's ever come in her life.

"Don't look at *me*," she says.

"Steph, you can't use American appliances in Europe. They're the wrong voltage or wattage or something."

"What do you know about it, anyway?"

"It was in one of those folders we got: 'Tips for Foreign Visitors.'"

"I'm not foreign," Steph explains. *"They're* foreign. I didn't read that stuff. I didn't even want to come."

"But you knew you were going to."

"But I didn't *want* to."

That's the kind of logic you can't argue with, especially since it's always worked for her before. For some reason I remember Mom saying, *Just get her there. Your grandmother will do the rest.* But that doesn't cover today.

I loll back in the chair, trying for a new approach. "Look, maybe this whole deal won't be so bad."

She makes a little tick sound back in her throat, and looks aside, truly bitter.

"You're always wanting Mom off your case. Well, she's off. She's about four thousand miles that way." I point in a convincing direction.

I see a flash of something in Steph's eyes. Fear? But she blinks it away.

"Actually, I like Mom," I say. Actually, I'm suddenly homesick . . . a vicious, sharp attack when I wasn't looking. Here I am on the wrong side of the world, face to face with Prudence Puberty, and time isn't passing like it should, and we just got here. "Actually, I love her."

"Why not?" Steph says, not moving her lips. "She lets you do anything you want."

A big lie, but I'm not messing with Steph's logic again. Why aren't I older? I wonder this a lot, but especially now. Then I'd know how to deal with

Steph, except Mom's never found the answer either. Age probably doesn't have anything to do with it. I don't see any end to this. When Steph's eighty-eight, she'll still be mature for her age, and I'll be a ninety-year-old geek.

With nothing to lose that I can think of, I decide to be Mr. Cool. "Anyway, we'll see the world."

Steph looks up. She'd had the time to do a Cyndi Lauper paint job on her eyes before she nuked the hotel. "The world doesn't have anything to do with me."

This seems to be her final word. Unconsciously, she draws a line with a finger on her side of the greasy table, a little wall line, fencing her in from the rest of the world. It's the best she can do four thousand miles from her room.

Her gaze shifts past me. She's facing the front door of the place, and her eyes get bigger, enormous. Is she seeing an English ghost? Are the hotel people coming for us? Has it just dawned on her that we're about to set sail on a ship full of the same gray-headed people who were on the bus? Does she—gasp—want her mother?

The people she's watching are coming past our table, and Steph's staring holes in them. Even her chair's turning. I look up to see three creatures from outer space. They're punkers. No, they're way past punk-as-we-know-it. They're also pretty far from any definite sexual identity. The first one seems about seven feet tall. Half of its hair, Day-Glo orange, is standing up like an enraged porcupine. The other half is shaved skull except for a red-and-blue square that may be the British flag.

The second one's face is divided down the middle, neatly between the nostrils. One half is painted flame red with flames, and white eyebrow, half-mouth, cheek. The other half's the reverse, red on white. The hair's dreadlocks, no two the same color, like the rainbow in an oil slick.

The third punker's got your basic Mohawk, though green, and is wearing an evening gown, orange, under a combat jacket. They all make a lot of noise as they move: chains, safety pins, studded leather bracelets, rhinestone brooches, metal cleats on their boots, earrings. A lot of earrings.

Steph's mouth is open. She's run a hand up to one of her ears. She's got three puny little gold hoops in that ear, and a single pearl in the other one. The punkers have this much hardware in their noses. She blinks, remembering her eyes: a little pale purple and washed-out yellow—nothing. Kid stuff.

I lead her back to the hotel, and she lets me. By the time we get there, the lights are back on. They've gotten the place rewired, or whatever it took.

There are notes under our door that night . . . from the beautiful escort? . . . that tell us to leave all our luggage, packed, in the hallway. It'll be picked up in the middle of the night and trucked down to the ship for us.

I pack up and decide to sleep in my T-shirt and Jockeys. I hit the bed and start to die. No point in waiting for it to get dark outside, which it doesn't seem to do.

Vaguely, I sense Steph in my room again. "Something's wrong with my TV," she says. "It only gets four channels."

I'm nearly in the Land of Nod, but when Steph wants her MTV, she wants her MTV. "Maybe that's all the channels they have."

I hear the tick in her throat. Then she calls England a really gross name. Should I remind her that this is the last TV she'll be seeing for quite a while? Nahhh. Then I die.

I wake up, unjet-lagged, morning sun beaming in. It's a little after eight, and we're supposed to be on the bus with the gray-heads by nine sharp. I climb into my boots and yesterday's clothes and wash my teeth, using hotel toothpaste and my index finger because I've packed my toothbrush. I consider shaving, but I never have, and there's no need to start now. From the next room I hear Steph in the shower, so we seem to be rolling.

They bring up breakfast without even being asked. A pot of tea; toast, cold and stony; strange pale orange juice. At quarter to nine I see the bus down on the street, gray-heads streaming in. I'm in no hurry. I even have a small plan about not sitting with Steph.

She explodes into my room, airborne. Also she seems to think she's wrapped in a hotel towel, but it's flapping loose. She's this shapeless, quivering figure in training bra and flowered bikini pants. Her eyes are bulging like the madwoman she probably is. Raising both fists, she screams.

It's deafening. You picture Big Ben keeling over.

"Steph. What?"

"Look at me!" She grabs the towel around her so I won't. "Look at meeeee!"

Awareness comes to me in a blinding flash. When she put her packed luggage out in the hallway, she packed *all* her clothes in it, except what she happens to have on right now, which couldn't get her anywhere but arrested. She hadn't saved anything to wear today. She hadn't thought ahead because, after all, she doesn't even want to be here. It's also the first time she's ever obeyed an order, and look where it's gotten her . . . naked in a foreign country.

"Do something!" she screams.

Like what? The luggage went by truck to the ship in the middle of the night, just like they said it would. I've got to take charge here, but I can't resist shrugging once and turning my palms up in the air. This sends her decibels off the charts. She's beginning to do a war dance in bare feet. She must have packed her Reeboks along with everything else.

42

"Chill out, Steph," I yell over her shrieks. "I'll find the BE."

She sobers suddenly. "What's that?"

"The Beautiful Escort," I say, and go looking for her.

We have a busy fifteen minutes. The BE is supposed to be helping oldsters onto the bus. But it seems Steph isn't the first traveler who ever made this small mistake. Though she's the first one who wasn't senile.

The BE and I go racing around the hotel. She's got a change of clothes of her own in her office. To get there we plunge down a back hall where the hotel maids hang out. I picture borrowing one of their uniforms and watching Steph, who's never made her own bed, going up the gangplank disguised as a servant. It's just a passing fantasy. The BE throws her extra clothes in my arms and reminds us we'd better not miss the boat, or the bus to it.

I charge back upstairs, dump everything into Steph's naked arms. She darts into her room, and time passes. Too much time passes. Down on the street, I hear the bus motor idling.

"Steph?"

Nothing.

I go into her room, and at first it looks empty. Then I see her standing in the corner like a dress dummy for a fire sale.

"I'm not going," she says.

The BE's extra clothes are another uniform: very grown up, which is what Steph thinks she is. White blouse, blue blazer with Regal Cruise Line crest, gray flannel skirt, black high-heeled shoes. The BE looks great in this. The BE is also around five seven, with a bust, waist, hips, legs, ankles, a lot of good stuff. Steph's five one. Period.

The blouse looks okay on her. That's about all. The blazer is way out of proportion. It nips in just at Steph's widest. The skirt's a disaster from top to bottom. Because of a long-term Doritos addiction, Steph is a little thick in the middle. The skirt's cutting her in two. She looks like she's expecting something other than a cruise. The skirt just clears her ankles, bare because I didn't deliver pantyhose. She's into the high-heeled shoes with room to spare, and she's swaying like a tree.

"I'm not going," she says, and stamps her foot with an odd clumping sound. "I can't go like this. I'm not going."

Downstairs the bus guns in neutral. Steph looks toward the window—thinking of jumping? But she's not about to move. I have one of my rare breakthrough solutions. Timing is everything. I leap at her, a giant jump.

"Quick," I yell right in her ear, grabbing her hand. "We've got to get out of here *now*." I start running, dragging her, and I keep yelling. She was about to have hysteria anyway, so why not make it work for us?

The one thing she didn't pack was her purse. I detour past the bed and grab it up for her. I already have my billfold and passport in my pants pocket. I aim us at the door and run her through it. She's almost dead weight, but I've panicked her. If we wait for the elevator, she'll have time to think, or get away. We start pounding down the fire stairs.

This is Steph's first trip anywhere in high-heeled shoes. On the bare stairs she sounds like heavy metal. She's gasping in my ear, and her hand's turning in my fist. Her other arm's flailing, trying to reach for something solid, but we're moving too fast. We hit the lobby at our top speed, and people scatter, making way.

She starts to fall down the steps outside, but we don't have time for that. I've developed one of Schwarzenegger's arms. I keep her going. We both rocket onto the bus. The door hisses shut behind us, and we move out.

We're both wringing wet. The bow on Steph's blouse is around under her ear. Only her fingertips are sticking out from her sleeves. Her feet are no doubt killing her.

"I hate you, Drew," she says, getting her breath back. "I always have, and especially lately."

But her heart isn't in it. She flops into the nearest seat, looking like the Incredible Shrinking Woman.

Next to her is an old gent who probably thinks she's an official Regal Cruise Line escort, dwarf division. And in another hour, we'll be at Tilbury Docks, and the big ship, and Grandmother, who's this person we don't really know.

Chapter 4

Regal Voyager; flagship of Regal Cruise Lines; Panamanian registry and Greek crew; 32,740 tons; 785 feet long, 90 feet at beam; 812 passengers; crew of 435; cruising speed of 24 knots. 264 outside cabins, 129 inside, and ten suites.

Amenities include indoor and outdoor pools, movie theater, full Nautilus health club, shopping arcade, modest library. Dining facilities: the Magellan (main) dining room with early and late seatings, the Galleon buffet on the Promenade Deck, and the Café Athena for informal dining. Principal public rooms: the Calypso Club (disco), the Adriatica Room (nightly variety acts), La Panoramique (ballroom), and El Morocco (casino).

Despite a sleek, modern image, this ship attracts a faithful following of mainly elderly, conservative passengers.

It's incredible—standing eleven stories above the Thames River, looking too solid to float. People going up the gangway look like mice.

Steph and I are a couple of the mice. She's clunking up the incline, and we're not speaking. Officer types in white uniforms and gold-braid caps hand us inside. How are we supposed to spot Grandmother in this mob? Half the passengers are grandmothers. With only our assigned numbers to go on, we manage to find our cabins. We're six flights down on Coral Deck, pretty much water level.

My cabin's not exactly Love Boat. You could only swing half a cat in it, and the narrow bed drops out of the wall. No porthole. But there's a midget bathroom. In fact, it looks like we're down with the hired help, which we are. The best part is that my big suitcase and the flight bag have already been delivered.

Steph sees my stuff, sighs, and turns to her room across the hall. There's no key in her door, but it's unlocked. I notice her luggage on the floor in there before she bangs the door behind her. It's a pretty solid bang, so she may settle in here yet. I'm thinking about unpacking when I hear her . . . through two closed doors. Not quite a scream; more of an amplified whine. I pay her a call before she draws a crowd.

She's already yanked off her borrowed blazer. There's plenty of room in the front of the blouse, and the tight-waisted skirt makes her look like the Pillsbury Doughboy.

"Look at this place." She slaps the side of her own head.

The place is bigger than mine—two beds, in fact. A closet with an open door is already full of clothes: evening gowns, beaded stuff, possibly a fur piece, feathers even. There are a lot of shoes around, little high-heeled ones, too small for Steph. They're lined up under one of the beds on their little platform soles, and they're heaped on the closet floor. There's a perfumy smell in here. The dressing table's covered with powder boxes, cotton balls, eye pencils.

Steph's pointing at a picture, a big faded photograph in a frame by the mirror. It's a picture of Grandmother, the way she used to look, with an orchid on her shoulder. She's with a young guy in an army uniform and service cap. They're both smiling, showing teeth. It could be an ancient wedding picture.

Steph grabs her hand back, because tucked behind the picture is a life-size plastic head without features. It's got a wig on. Actually, it's got three wigs on. They look like a trio of shaggy little forest creatures stacked up and asleep.

Steph's head is back, eyes filling with tears. What we've got here is a disaster in the making. She's going to have to share quarters with Grandmother. Steph, whose room back home is Forbidden City—the Temple of Doom for anybody who even drops in.

"And you have your own room," she whispers.

It's true. I turn up my palms.

"This is the worst day of my life," Steph says. "I thought yesterday was, but it wasn't."

More or less on cue, the door opens behind me. A huge, grinning jack-o'-lantern face appears, and speaks.

"Hi, keeds. I am Stavros, your steward. You wan some Greek soda pop? Is better than American. Is better than Coke, Poopsie, Sprint, Dr Peeper. Is Greek."

"I want to die," Steph says.

But Stavros doesn't pick up on that. "Good choice!" he says, and disappears.

I have a feeling we'll be seeing a lot of Stavros. I don't say so to Steph because she really doesn't like people coming into her room, or have I mentioned that?

She's truly mad now, bending over her carry-on case and littering the place with her stuff until she finds her hair dryer. Then she whips around and jams the plug into a wall socket. The dryer begins to whir in her hand, normally. She stares down at it, turning the business end of it up to blow hot air in her face. Was she only checking to see if it would work, or was she hoping to short out the ship, maybe send us to the bottom? Better not ask.

"You probably won't be spending much time in here anyway," I tell her. "Why don't you change out of those . . . clothes, and we'll check out the ship."

Then I wait for Steph to decide. Whether to explore the ship with her geeky brother who she hates or wait in this phone booth for the grandmother, who wears wigs. Like Steph says, it's the worst day of her life. And we haven't sailed yet.

We get lost on every deck. We find both swimming pools, but they turn out to be the same one. It's Monopoly, and we keep passing Go. The halls are blocked with passengers still finding their rooms and stewards delivering flowers. We find the Magellan Room, and it's a soccer field set for dinner. It doesn't look like it's going to serve our type of food. The headwaiter spots us, and we vanish. We keep having to retrace our steps. If we were to go to the purser's office, we could get a deck plan, but we don't know what a purser is.

You can hear music all over the ship. In the El Morocco area, they haven't started gambling yet, but there's a pianist taking requests. In La Panoramique, a three-piece string group is playing slow-dance numbers. A few senior citizens are on their feet, slowly revolving, dipping even. We stare. We've never seen people this age dancing.

By chance, we stumble onto the Adriatica Room, a big nightclub. It's got tables on levels looking down on a low stage in front of a bandstand. Overhead there's a lot of high-tech lighting. The band's rehearsing, a ten-man outfit including the old guy on piano. We stop just inside the entrance, a long way from them.

The band leader's Marty Wilhelm of the Wilhelm Melodiers, according to the sign on the drum. He doubles in brass and conducts with a trumpet.

Or maybe he only thinks he's leading. A small woman's sitting on a high stool in the middle of the floor with her back to the band and a score in her lap. Her feet don't begin to reach the floor. They're propped up, hooked onto a rung by high heels. She's wearing a pantsuit and big dark glasses. She puts one little arm in the air and snaps her fingers. It stops the song cold.

"Let's hear that sax by himself," she says—not loud, but they hear. "Sounds flat to me. Last four bars."

We hear the sax again, and she concentrates, listening.

"Right," she says. "Better."

They're ready to go on, but she says, "Let's try the drummer on brushes instead of sticks."

He switches over, and she adds, "Nice piano."

Then the band blares, and the lights go from yellow to pink. Behind her the sound softens, and she begins to sing.

"I tremble . . . this near your arms . . ."

It's not a big voice. It just fills up the room exactly. I happen to notice there's no mike, not even pinned into her clothes.

"... I tremble ... this near your charms ...
   Why do I feel this way?
     Why don't you go away?
      Why aren't there words to say. ..."

I know by now who she is. Who else could it be? It's just that we found her, she didn't find us.

I even seem to know that she's seen us, behind her big dark glasses. But she has a song and a band to rehearse. The glasses hide her eyes. Her hair's as black as in her old pictures, but bigger. She's almost too tiny for a grown-up, but she's not a little old lady. She's Connie Carlson.

A blast vibrates through the room. Steph and I leap. It's the ship's horn, rattling glasses in the bar. You can feel it in your feet. The band blunders on, even though the ship is roaring a hundred times louder. When it stops, she's still right there, hitting every note.

"... On nights like this,
   I tremble for your lips to kiss,
     For times alone,
      The ringing of the telephone,

And days and nights, a lifetime lost
In your arms. . . ."

Her hand comes up at the end, just a little gesture.
I notice she's saving some things for the real performance and wonder how I know that.

In the last bars of the song, the ship begins to move.
You can hardly tell when, but somewhere up on deck
another band's playing. Twisted ticker-tape blows
past the windows of the Adriatica Room. She turns on
the stool, toward the band. "Thanks, fellas. We'll get
through it."

They put their instruments down, not even looking at their official leader, I notice. What we have
here is a very up-front lady. Now she wants us up
front. She saw us when we came in. Now she's ready
for us. She points at us and crooks a finger. Beside me,
Steph shudders. Then we start down the long,
carpeted tiers. We have to.

When she slips off the stool, I tower over her. In
high heels, Steph would too.

As soon as she takes off her dark glasses, I begin
searching her for clues . . . links. I don't see much
in her face that reminds me of Mom. Of course
they're both very programed, but that's about it.
Grandmother's eyes are the young ones in her picture, still made up like the 1940s, each curled lash
separate and the brows painted on. She's looking us
over—sizing us up? Her lips are painted on, too, and

54

she purses them. Maybe she doesn't know where to begin. Neither do I. My, how we've grown, but she doesn't say so.

Her hands start out to us, but she pulls them back. She turns to pick up her music, clutches it instead of us.

". . . Well," she says, "well." She doesn't know where to begin, and neither do I. "And how are things at home?"

"Mom's fine."

I want to add: *She'd like to have come,* but I don't. I think of saying, *She sends you her love,* but she didn't. Grandmother's eyes linger over us. Either she wants to hear more, or we're a couple of packages she's forgotten she ordered. She glances at Steph, studies her, maybe looking for links herself.

But Steph's staring somewhere out in space. Her lower lip is out a mile, and her eyes are marble hard. I know Steph. With adults, she likes to establish her authority first. She also has a major bone to pick about having to share her room. She's got so many complaints, she doesn't know where to begin. But Grandmother turns away from her, back to the bandstand. She's a lot more comfortable in her world than with us. It could be a long voyage.

Though most of the musicians are beginning to leave, there's still time to introduce them to her grandchildren, but she doesn't. She puts up a finger to keep us in place, and goes back to the old piano player. Bending over him, she shuffles through his music, has a few words with him. She pats him on the arm, lightly, and strolls back to us.

She's one strong lady, a tiny power-pack. I can almost feel something like heat radiating off her, though she's cool. And while she's no particular age, she makes me feel like I ought to be older, like you can't afford to be too young around her.

"We've picked up a new man on piano, and we're working him in. The fella we had on the last cruise had trouble with 'Chopsticks.' I've worked in front of better bands."

She smiles a little. Above the painted-on lips the skin is accordion pleated in fine wrinkles, but her cheeks are smooth, powdered. "I'm lucky to be working at all. I'm sixty-four years old. And I may have knocked off a couple of years."

She plants her little fists on her sides. "Ancient?"

". . . Ah, oh, no," I say. Suave.

"Sure it is. In this business a girl singer's ancient at *thirty*-four. That makes me prehistoric. I knew Dinah Shore before Holly Farms chicken. I knew Doris Day when her name was Kappelhoff. I knew Sinatra with hair."

She strolls away, and I guess we're supposed to follow. We're heading back down to our rooms, and we don't take the elevator because she's spry and wants us to see that.

"A good trip?" she asks.

I mentally review a few highlights, from the time-warp plane flight, to the hair dryer as a lethal weapon, to the punked-out McDonald's, to Steph in orbit in her training bra.

"Fine trip," I say. "Pretty routine."

"And you're settled in?" Grandmother says, meaning the staterooms.

Steph's already speechless with rage, and this is the last straw. She's not speaking to either of us, permanently. Her jaw's clamped, and she's stalking along in her Reeboks.

"And let's see, Stephanie," Grandmother remarks. "You'd be thirteen?"

It's the one question in the universe Steph would have to answer. "Fourteen."

"Oh, heavens," Grandmother says, strolling along. "At your age I was making my own living. I cut my first record at fifteen. On the Decca label."

I have to grin. I can't help it. Then we're down on good old Coral Deck, our neighborhood.

"And by the way," Grandmother says. "Call me Connie. Everybody does."

Gran—Connie does two shows that night, the cocktail one and the after-dinner, with a somewhat noisier crowd. The Adriatica Room holds five hundred people, and she fills it twice, so some people come for both shows.

Steph and I are there each time, though not up front at ringside. We're still hanging around at the back, still not ready to commit. We've changed clothes, but we're still casual. Steph's wearing a sweatshirt that reads:

THERE IS NO GRAVITY
THE WORLD SUCKS

Her statement, but I notice she's here, not holed up in her half of the room.

The cruise director acts as MC, welcoming everybody on the first night of the cruise, telling us all what a great trip we're going to have. Then a magician opens the show—Milo the Magnificent. He's good, but about fifty and so a little young for this crowd.

The Wilhelm Melodiers do a couple of sets, and people get up to dance. In fact the band sounds better in a full room with tinkling glasses and waiters dropping the occasional tray. Then it's time for Connie. People sit down, get quiet.

Just before she comes on, it dawns on me that she isn't prehistoric for this audience. She's one of them, their idea of a star, the last of the stars. Even the lights say so. The Adriatica Room washes lavender and then pink, and it's a nightclub forty-five years ago. Everybody's young again, and we've got a war to win.

The cruise director doesn't announce her. A pinpoint of pale pink light finds her face as she enters next to the piano. She's just there. And once again, I don't know her.

From here it doesn't look like a wig, and her eyelashes look real. She's wearing a black lace dress, bare
on one shoulder, and she's carrying a long scarf. Her
fingernails are enormously long, enormously red.
The dress is fairly short, and she's wearing a pair of
her high-heeled shoes. Even without them, she'd
look normal size, even somewhat larger than life.
She's amazing. Not beautiful, just amazing. The pink-
ish lights wash away the years from her face and
shoulder. Her legs are silky, perfectly proportioned. I
nudge Steph.

"Did you see her getting into all that?"

Steph's staring at her. She nods.

The place goes crazy. You wouldn't think people
this old could make so much noise. Connie's blotted
out. The men stand up first, clapping over their
heads, walling us away from her. Then the women
are up, waving high in the pink air.

But they sit down again pretty quick because they
want to hear her. There's a little sway in her hips as
she rounds the grand piano and fits herself into the
curve of it. She smiles, and the pink lights go warmer.
In fact she's warmer than in real life, except for her
this is real life.

"Who knows," she says, and they start screaming,
"where or when?" It's the name of a song, and she
sings it. There's something smoky in her voice,
young. She takes her time with it, bows her head to

59

the old piano player in the middle of it, and he plays part of the refrain alone. Then she finishes.

She strolls to center stage. "Well, where was it?" she says to everybody individually, "Where and when were we last together? Was it . . . the Paramount in New York?"

Applause bursts.

"Or was it the old Palomar Ballroom out in L.A.?"

Voices call out.

"Was it the Glen Island Casino up in New Rochelle?" Connie wonders, "or the Meadowbrook down in Cedar Grove?

"Were any of you jitterbuggers there the night we opened the Shamrock Hotel in Houston?"

The Texans in the crowd holler and stomp.

"And what about the Aragon Ballroom in Chicago—"

"No, the Trianon!" an old guy yells out. "Nineteen forty-one, Connie!"

"I was there," she says, "singing songs like these."

She goes into a set, and they'd like to applaud every song, but they don't want to interrupt her. We move at her pace. In the last song of the set she strolls around the edge of the stage, taking people's hands, making contact.

When she finishes, they want to give her another standing ovation, but she says, "I stole most of those songs from better singers. I borrowed 'Sunday Kind of Love' from Fran Warren and 'My Heart Belongs to

Daddy' from Kitty Kallen and 'I Don't Want to Walk Without You' from Helen Forrest. I stole 'What Is This Thing Called Love' from Mel Tormé and the Meltones."

They laugh, clap. They don't believe it. They think all these songs belong to Connie. "Oh, yes, that was my career, going from band to band, with a little radio work to fill in. I took over for Kay Starr with Charlie Barnet, and I took over for Peggy Lee with Benny Goodman. I lived through the greatest of times, and I had the greatest of times.

"Wasn't I lucky? Weren't we all? The big bands came along to dance us out of the Depression. And they were there when we marched off to war. We went to war ourselves, and some of us didn't come back. Glenn Miller didn't come back."

The room's suddenly silent, reverent.

"Then one day our kind of music was over. But wasn't it swell while it lasted? Like all the stories in the storybooks we were about love and laughter and happily-ever-after. We were about good times and not so good times, and how your memories never let you grow old."

Everything's mellow now, even the lighting, and people are quiet. They seem to be sitting closer together. She's talking to them heart to heart, but I wonder if she's telling Steph and me who she is. I wonder if she's looking for us as she glances around the room. Or maybe she's just counting the house.

She breaks her own mood with something sudden
in her face, and the lighting. She goes into another
set, her big finish. It's songs from World War II.
"There'll Be Bluebirds over the White Cliffs of Do-
ver," "I Left My Heart at the Stagedoor Canteen,"
"Praise the Lord and Pass the Ammunition," and a
couple more I don't pick up on. And in the fast ones
she begins to move. Her foot starts to tap, and she's
going at it, her hands in the air, her head back, her
scarf whipping the air. She's whipping up the audience too. They're dancing in place, even with each
other. I never saw people this . . . happy.

Then it's over except for the encore, and they have
to ask for it. She turns back to the curtains, but she
isn't going anywhere. People start yelling the word.
"Swingtime."

She pivots around and lays it on them. She's all
over the stage with it. Her little shoes begin to blur
The lights play across her face in two colors, like
cherry blossoms down in Dixie.

She comes to the end, grows still. "Yes," she says,
" 'Swingtime Down in Dixie' really was my song. Not
bad for a girl from Milwaukee."

They love it, but she's suddenly smaller. It's over,
and they know it. She takes her bows, does some
business with the scarf, acknowledges the band, and
begins to move away. But she turns back at the curtains and silences them with a look.

"Do nothing till you hear from me," she says, and

they roar because that's one of her big numbers, and she always holds something back for next time.

Between shows we have something to eat with her in the lounge. "I work better on a full stomach," she says. "Mine was empty too often."

At the end of the evening, late, we walk her back to the room, going the long way low in the ship to avoid the fans. She takes my arm, it's the first time we've touched. She's leaning on me, though I don't think she notices, and teetering on her ridiculous shoes. I look down to see she's too exhausted to speak. She's given them all she's got—twice. Out of the pink light, she's older, old. She goes on ahead of Steph into their small and littered cabin. Weirdly, Steph closes the door quietly behind them.

I turn the key in my door and stand inside in the dark. The beat of the old-fashioned band is still throbbing lightly in my head. I run over a few current events. I happen to be on the far side of the world and six flights down. My grandmother turns out to be the Madonna of her particular generation. And this really isn't the kind of summer I had in mind.

I have to admit it's different. I scan back over the other adults in my life: Mom, Mr. Morthland, the teachers at school. They all seem to be there for the convenience of kids. I mean, where would they be without us?

I don't know about Connie. She's in business for

herself, and I didn't know adults were. This could be a major breakthrough in my thinking.

But I'm too tired for thought. I flip on the light. There on the table is a glass of melted ice and a sweating bottle. I guess Stavros ran out of Greek soda pop. It's Poopsie.

Chapter 5

The day begins with the *Regal Voyager* newsletter slipped under the door. It tells everything, even how to dress for dinner. There's a complete rundown of shipboard activities: the aerobics class, duplicate bridge, the computer clinic, Rotary Club, the movie times, the dance lessons, shuffleboard, skeet shooting, blackjack, bingo, and five meals a day if you can handle them. Talk about a total life-support system.

Breakfast is over on the side in the Magellan Room. We have our own waiter, Nico, and a menu three feet long of breakfast specialties. We eat with the help: the cruise director's staff, the London people who run the gambling games, the musicians from all the bands except you don't see much of them at breakfast, and all the other entertainers. Thirty or forty people at long tables, acting pretty much like family. It's sort of interesting being on the inside.

The three of us come in to breakfast together. Connie's wigless head is wrapped in a scarf like a turban, and she's wearing one of her pantsuits. She's back behind her dark glasses where it's hard to find her, and she looks like a night's sleep didn't do her much good. A few passengers manage to spot her. They speak, reach out to her as we pass by. There are even a few patterings of applause.

Steph pokes me. I glance down. She's looking okay: no junk on her eyes, but not too molelike.

"Sit with me," she hisses.

Steph wanting to sit with me? "Why?"

"I don't know any of these people." Worse, they're all adults.

"Look, my job was to get you here," I say. "Now you're on your own." This is talking a language she understands. She's into rejection herself so she snuggles up to me.

Connie introduces us to the group and taps the middle of three empty chairs. I pull it back for her because Nico's coming up on us at a gallop but isn't quick enough. I seat Connie, and I'd even seat Steph, but she flops down too quick.

"Eat up," Connie says, running a long red fingernail down her menu and stopping at hash browns. "I'm singing for our supper."

It takes me a while to notice I'm sitting next to a porthole. There's nothing out there but sea and sky. In a ship this big, you could wander for days and never find the ocean. It's the North Sea at this point, and I'm amazed all over again at being here. The breakfast is great, the best. Nico keeps checking back, wondering if everything's all right and would we rather have something else?

Pigging out, I hardly notice someone leaning over to speak to Connie. Maybe I get a whiff of something . . . English lavender? Then a hand falls on my shoulder, light as a feather. I notice these long, tapering fingers festooning my collarbone. I look up and feel faint.

"Hello," she says, British in the first two syllables. "I'm called Holly . . . the dance instructress?"

I don't care if you're named Beulah and you stoke the boilers. This is the most beautiful human being I've ever seen. I have a nearly uncontrollable urge to put my hand up and pat my shoulder. She's beyond belief. She makes the BE back in London look like an Airedale.

"You're Andrew."

". . . Just . . . Drew." My voice starts changing all over. I seem to be reentering seventh grade.

First of all, she has red hair and skin like—what? Seashells? Pearls? You tell me. I'm going blind. Her eyes are green. I've never actually seen green eyes before. She seems to be wearing a leotard under a big white shirt loosely tied at an unbelievable waist. I want to stand back and really see her. But I'm hedged in by my grandmother, my breakfast, and the North Sea.

"At the cha-cha-cha lesson, we're always short of men."

Men. That's *me*. She wants me at her cha-cha-cha lesson. My tongue's tight against the roof of my mouth, but I nod. I don't know what cha-cha-cha is, but I've been thinking of majoring in it.

"Eleven o'clock sharp," Holly says. "La Panoramique." She moves away, doubtless like a dancer. But I'm staring at my plate. I've got an hour and a half to kill. How?

"Cha-cha-cha," Connie murmurs, but when I look at her, she's dabbing her little pursed lips with a napkin—innocent.

Suddenly, I happen to notice my body. I don't know why. It's always been there. I've got this concave chest I can't seem to do anything about. It's under a golf shirt that I've got faded just right, but I need to do something about my arms if I'm going to wear short sleeves. I've got on my white Levi's— fresh, since this is the first day. My legs are too thin. I don't know. I eat a lot. Where do I put it? But I'm five nine and three quarters. Five ten and a half if I practice good posture. Over six foot if I stand on something. It's not bad. I've been shorter. Michael J. Fox is only five four. Maybe I'll grow some more on this cruise. No. I'm a grown man already. Without giving it enough thought, I turn to Connie.

"Did you tell . . . anybody how old I am?"

She's ready. She turns two black lenses on me. "On a cruise, you're any age you can get away with."

Oh.

I look out the porthole at the sea and sky. Suddenly the possibilities seem limitless.

As it turns out, I don't have any time to kill. We have lifeboat drill, not an elective. They have to hold it within twenty-four hours of sailing, and we all report to our lifeboats for inspection from the captain. We're wearing life jackets, bright orange and ridiculously puffy. Steph's there, though none too happy about it. On the other hand, the life jacket's giving her the figure she's been waiting for. We're on the enclosed deck, and our lifeboat hanging from a davit outside looks fairly seaworthy. I check down our rows to see who'd be with us in case we're ever cast adrift. I think maybe in an open boat, rowing for our lives, we could always use a dancing teacher. She isn't here.

At five to eleven in La Panoramique there are about twenty ladies of advanced years, four old guys, and me. I'm here early, not wanting to hold them up. Holly's here and, yes, she's wearing a leotard under the big shirt. Her shoes are a dancer's: good, thick heel with one strap across, well broken in.

She welcomes us, gives us the pitch. On our days at sea, we'll learn new dances. We'll nail the cha-cha-cha first. Then we'll master the samba, the rhumba.

We'll go on and on. I hear about these days ahead, and my mouth goes dry. It's like getting into the college of your choice.

I'm already trying to memorize her. Sturdy dancer legs, waist just two hands around, my hands. The fire of her hair, the emerald eyes, the swan's neck, the graceful arms.

"I shall need a partner," she says. One of her graceful arms reaches for a big old guy who's seventy if he's a day, in a cardigan sweater. But he may not be a bad choice. He takes her in his arms, and his elbows fly up. This could be the regulation cha-cha-cha position. Music blares from a tape: bouncy, South American rhythms. It's either sidestep, sidestep, sidestep, then you clap your hands and say cha-cha-cha. Or it's forward, forward, forward. I can't concentrate. I keep trying to see her face over the old guy's shoulder, but he's a bear. And he keeps grinning around at the rest of us. I don't grin back.

"Very good indeed," Holly says, skipping neatly out from under his size thirteens. "Quite promising."

She forms us up in a circle, except there are four women for every man, so we men have to keep moving ahead in the circle to give every woman a chance to dance. We move every time Holly claps her castanet. It's hard work. I'm sweating, and I've never had a dance lesson. I'm not due at the prom for another two years.

We go for an hour. I don't know how they do it. I'm

being danced to death by eighty-year-old women. They're serious about it. There's no conversation, and when they clap, they look grim.

Holly doesn't join in, which is fine. I'm getting big, crusty crescents of sweat under my arms, and I still can't get the hang of this dance. Then it's over, and everybody's fresh as a daisy except me. I drop into a big lounge chair, waiting to see if all the old cha-cha-cha pros go away and Holly doesn't. It happens.

"I was bad," I say, still winded.

She's busy rewinding the tapes, but she says, "Yes, I have never had an utter failure in the dance class, until today."

"Hey, wait, you didn't think I'd have music in my soul, or rhythm in my feet because of my grand-mother."

"I lived in hope," she says. "I assume you don't sing?"

"I was in middle-school chorus, but I dropped out."

"For the good of the group," Holly murmurs.

I love it, but my mind's gunning in neutral. I want to keep her talking, but I'm also trying to think. What is she? Nineteen? Okay, twenty, tops.

"Twenty-two last March," she remarks.

Fine, she reads minds on the side. And it's also fine because we're only five years apart, which is nothing in the years ahead. Because I'm seventeen. On a cruise ship you can be any age you can get away with. I have it on good authority.

She's finished with the tapes and comes over to sit down in the chair next to mine, curls up in it. I still don't have my breath back from the dancing, and this won't help. Here we are in an empty, floating ballroom, and out the portholes the snow-white ship knifes through the choppy waters of the endless sea. Is this happening?

I've got to keep up the momentum here. I open my mouth, hoping for automatic pilot. "Ah, I don't suppose you'd care to tell me the story of your life?"

"Wouldn't dream of it," she says, propping up her chin.

"I mean, do you work on the ship all the time?"

"Year round, except when we're in dry dock. On that month I go home to my parents who live in a twee cottage in Kent."

Twee? We have a language barrier to overcome, which is fine because I'm willing.

"And what's life on the ship like?"

She thinks. Is she about to put me on again?

"It's mostly a question of dealing with Americans, you see."

"What's that like?"

"Quite nice," Holly says, "but the important thing with Americans is never to take them too seriously. They're a bit like grown-up children."

Where does that leave me? "But . . . you like the job."

"Ummm," she says, nodding.

She says ummm when she means yes. Maybe this is English English. I'd say ummm to anything she cared to suggest.

"And Americans are terribly curious whilst the English are terribly private."

This could mean keep your nose out of my business, so I decide the next line is hers.

"And what's it like to be Miss Carlson's grandson?" she asks.

"I'm new on the job. We haven't spent much time with her before. I'm on with my sister."

"Ummm," Holly says. "I remember being that age. It was awful."

"You weren't as awful as Steph."

"I was worse. I had spots and was in love with my horse. We had to wear school uniforms, and I looked like a pillar box in mine."

"What's a pillar box?"

"A perfectly round receptacle for letters and postcards."

"You weren't as bad as Steph."

Which makes Holly laugh, and how can I do that again?

"At least I was spared an older brother."

At least she said *older.*

Subtle chimes chime for the first seating at lunch. But she never has lunch. She's a dancer and eats rabbit food in the quarters she shares with three other girls. I hear this explanation in waves of sound

73

because she's getting up to go, unwinding herself. And I don't have time to blink, or think. Dinner? But no, not tonight. She's working.

She's halfway to the door, moving straight spined, neat heeled. No extra little sways and flourishes for anybody who happens to be watching.

I hear myself saying a whole paragraph. "By the way, I forgot to mention I'm twenty-nine. Been pretty tied down with the commodities market the past few years, and, ah, grain futures. Way too busy to settle down, but I been thinking about it."

Where did that come from? Back in my brain, Bates Morthland is writhing on my behalf. *Cut yourself some slack on the verbal interfacing, man.*

Holly pivots perfectly. "What a relief," she breathes. "I only go for older men." Then she goes.

I'll see her again. We're on the same ship in the same ocean. Why am I panicked?

Chapter 6

I spend the afternoon in a blur on the top deck. It's incredible up here, really being at sea. Between the funnels is a glass-enclosed tennis court and past that a practically undiscovered open stretch covered with fake grass. It's out of the wind with a few deck chairs scattered around.

I strip down to my Speedos to get some rays. If I can't do anything else about my body, I can get some color on it. I'm the same shade as skim milk.

This is more like it. I have the sun for the body and Holly for my fantasies. This cruise isn't such a bad idea, and I'm glad I thought of it. I try to picture what Bates is doing about now, but there's a six- or seven-hour time difference that's hard to work out. I find I can't think about anything but right now. I doze.

When I wake up, the sun's dropping behind us. I

hear the murmur of girl-voices muffled by the steady sound of the wind. I have my deck chair flat, and I'm lying on my stomach, trying to get the sun on my shoulder blades where there's been a small episode of acne. I look up to see two chairs across the space, facing the other way. There are two female bodies in them. I notice bare flesh and skimpy swimsuits through the webbing on the chairs. One head's blondish and the other one's dark. I rule out Holly and somebody. These two are younger. Scraps of conversation waft my way.

"Can you believe it?" "Give me a break." "I'm so sure."

I feel pins and needles on my back, so I've had enough sun. Besides, something's dawning on me. I'm up in a crouch and advancing on the deck-chair backs, unseen.

Nearer, I see two pairs of legs stretched out and sopping with oil. One pair's thick and pale. The other pair's thin and tan already. The two heads are close, communicating. I can hear everything:

". . . So Gillian Bergner just calls me up like it's nothing and goes, 'Listen, Stephy, I had this opportunity, and, like, I couldn't pass it up, right? Because at camp there'll be, you know, high-school guys?' And then she goes, 'But it's cool because you're going to Europe or someplace, right?' "

"Omigod," says the other head, the dark one. *"Omigod."*

I retreat. Picking up my clothes, I dress in the elevator dropping to Coral Deck. Steph's found a friend.

It's formal night, and here's where my useless white dinner jacket comes in handy. Tonight's an extra fancy dinner and a big show. Connie's not in it. I figured she'd entertain every night, but it doesn't work that way. They've got a lot of talent on board, so she only performs twice, once the first night and again on the last, "Gala Night." In between, she's mainly a passenger and resident celebrity.

"Show business is mostly waiting," Connie says. "You're lucky if you aren't waiting tables."

I'm in my room, changing. In fact I'm changing into somebody else. I've only got a regular white dress shirt, but Stavros has found me a black butterfly bow-tie, possibly off a waiter. I don't know how to tie the tie, but Stavros does. Now he's gone, and I'm easing into the white dinner jacket, which Stavros has cut the tags off of.

Now I'm turning to the mirror on my closet door. There I am, double breasted and dazzling in the early stages of a tan. The dinner jacket comes with its own shoulders.

I smile at this stud, and he does me a favor and smiles back. We reach for our combs and run them through our hair. A little more sun, and we might bleach out, surfer style. Then I go casual and stick my right hand in my pants pocket. He goes casual and sticks his left hand in his pants pocket. I'm seventeen. He could be in college. We even exchange a few witticisms.

The door flies open, and it isn't Stavros, because he knocks. It's Steph in a shorty bathrobe and chubbette legs beginning to peel. Also high-top Reeboks. She forgot to pack bedroom slippers.

"Who do you think you're talking to?" She looks around.

". . . Stavros. He's here when you can't see him. He's everywhere."

She's not interested. "Trouble," she says, business-like, "*major* trouble." She hammers my door home with a mighty fist. She doesn't see I've transformed myself into a black-and-white movie starring Fred Astaire as me.

"What could be wrong?" I say. "You've got a new friend—on board."

She doesn't wonder how I know this. "Melanie Krebs," she breathes, "who is *so cool.* She goes to *private school* in West Palm Beach, *Florida.* She's been on this ship before, *a lot.* There's a designer hair-dressing salon on the ship, and she's already *been.* And she's *fifteen.*"

From the glimpse I got, Melanie's a thirteen-year-old early bloomer, but let that go.

"It's okay, though," says Steph, "because I told her I'd be sixteen next week."

"Hey, *I'll* be sixteen next week."

"You I didn't mention," Steph says.

For some reason there's a big box under her arm. She slams it down. *"Here's* the trouble."

I'm not giving her the satisfaction, so she has to lift the box lid, then part a lot of tissue paper. Even before I see what's in there, I notice small alterations in Steph. For one thing, her hair's tied up in a scarf, turban style like Connie's. For another, she's got new fingernails of amazing length. I don't notice them at first because they're painted light pink, not Connie's fire-engine red. But they really do something for Steph, who's a long-term dedicated nail-biter. She's not used to them yet, and they get in her way.

"Glad to see you're letting them grow."

She considers passing them off as real, but decides she can't. "Connie put them on me. She said she used to be a . . . nail biter too."

I give this some thought. After meeting Cool Melanie Krebs, Steph's willing to upgrade her image. Did Connie figure that out and then introduce the new nails? If so, her timing's good, and what does this have to do with the box?

It's a dress, a dark-blue formal . . . long. She lifts it out of the box and holds it at arm's length, instead of against herself.

Connie gave me a dinner jacket, and so she's bought Steph a formal for the same occasion. Gratitude's too much to expect from Steph, and if Mom had bought her something to wear—a barrette—

79

without consulting her, we'd have serious door-banging and possibly nuclear winter.

"I'm not wearing this thing," Steph says, "just because *she* wants me to." But she's wobbling. Already she knows not to throw anything in Connie's face, let alone a dress. We don't really know Connie. But we know she's not Mom. I try to peer into Steph's brain to see what's going on. It's a can of worms in there.

You don't pick out clothes for her because it's too childish and it puts power into adults' hands where it has no business. Still, Steph can't take her eyes off it. This is her first formal. And she's more years from the senior prom than I am, no matter what she might tell you.

She'll be thinking about Cool Melanie Krebs, too, her instant friend and Gillian Bergner summer-replacement. If this is as good as or better than what Melanie's wearing tonight, Steph might overlook the insult of being given an expensive gift.

"Who does she think she is, anyway?" Steph says, meaning Connie. But she's practically whispering, and her heart definitely isn't in it.

She can't take it back to the store either. We're at sea.

"Where's it from?" I ask, just trying to help out.

Steph buys nothing anywhere but at Northbrook Court mall, the center of civilization. We both check out the box lid, which reads LIBERTY'S OF LONDON.

Somehow this doesn't sound like K mart. But Steph

shrugs. Still, she can't take her eyes off the dress. She's holding it up by the sleeves, and she's not sure it should have sleeves. On the other hand, she's remembering the zit on her left shoulder. At least she might be. She's got one there. Now she's looking at the front of the dress. There's some buildup just under the neckline. My dinner jacket has shoulders of its own. Her dress has its own bosom, or whatever you call it.

This pushes Steph over the edge. "Oh, well, I guess I'll have to wear it once," she says, seeming to do me a favor. "She got me shoes to go with it, silver sandals with a two-inch heel."

This is a big consideration. In two-inch heels, Steph will look like a lanky midget.

"She wrote Mom to get my sizes." Her eyes narrow at the thought of two grown women conniving behind her back. But she doesn't cram the dress back into the box. She folds it neatly in a way that reminds me of Mom. Steph's changing, just a little. It's like that movie, *The Fly*, except Steph's moving slightly *toward* humanity. By the end of the cruise, she might make it all the way to . . . but let's not get our hopes up.

She turns to go, and two steps will take her out the door. But she says, "Just do me one favor, right?"

"What."

"I'm moving into this room with you. I'll bring

over my stuff after the show tonight. You got an outlet for the hair dryer in here?"

"Hold it."

"Why not?" she says in her old whine.

"For a start, there's only one bed in here."

"You—I can sleep on the floor." She stubs my carpet with her Reebok.

"Steph, let me get this straight. At home, I'm not supposed to come into your room. Here, you want to *live* in mine?"

"I'd do it for you." With an argument like that, she must be desperate. "Besides, Connie snores."

"Be real, Steph."

". . . I'm scared." She blurts it out, surprising us both.

Scared? But she has her reasons. It's only the second day out, and already she's falling into Connie's hands. She's knuckling under. Steph's world is turning upside down. If she keeps doing what adults want her to do, she could end up back in childhood.

"Sorry, Steph." I almost am.

She only shrugs, hopeless, and leaves. She wasn't that crazy about rooming with me either.

The dinner's spectacular, even for here. There's an ice swan with a dripping beak on every table, flowers everywhere, the works. The whole menu's in French, so I'm at Nico's mercy and eat snails before I find out.

We've even got a rabbit, a live one, hopping down

the table, trying to eat the centerpiece. It belongs to Milo the Magician, who recaptures it and puts it away somewhere behind his lapels. The rabbit's in show business too. His name is Stu. I'm beginning to settle in here. But I scan down the employees' tables and don't see Holly. Did I dream her?

Steph's not here either. She's not sure about the dress, the shoes. She doesn't want Connie around while she's getting ready. She'll pass up dinner and meet us for the show.

"I wanted to help her get dressed," says Connie, next to me, "though that's the way girls are, I guess." But she reels in a waiter. "Nico, send down a tray of dinner for my granddaughter."

And Nico gives his all-purpose answer, which is, *"No problema."*

Personally, I don't think it would hurt Steph to miss a meal, but I don't say so.

It's a somewhat different Connie here at the table tonight. When she was rehearsing, she was all business. When she was performing, she was warm. Off-stage, she was smaller, drawn back. Now she's—a lady having dinner. Her outfit's plainer than the one she did her show in, but her dress is long, and there's a fur draped over her chair. She's in her number-two wig and another pair of tinted glasses with bright stones in the frames. It occurs to me these aren't star's glasses. They're prescription lenses—bifocals, in fact. She only does without her specs onstage. She's blind as a bat.

We're dinner partners, but she plays to the whole table: the magician, the comedian, both assistant cruise directors, the duplicate bridge teachers, the accordionist, and, down at the end, the old piano player, who's new on the job.

Still, she lays her hand on the arm of my dinner jacket. Little hand, mile-long red nails against my snow-white sleeve. I notice she doesn't wear rings. We have wine, and she doesn't wonder if I'm old enough. Tonight I'm old enough. We touch glasses, and she's a little shy, like a first date—though how would I know?

I bumble around, thanking her for the dinner jacket. She looks away from my words, but then she says, "You'll remember this. You'll remember this old lady who made you go on a ship once and dressed you up and gave you wine and made you listen to her warble. You'll tell *your* grandchildren about that summer and that crazy old broad, your grand-mother."

"I won't tell them a thing," I say. "I'll show them."

She cocks her head, and one eyebrow seems painted higher than the other one.

"I'll bring my grandchildren on the ship, and if they don't want to come, I'll beat them with belts," I tell her. "They can see you for themselves. Seeing's believing."

Connie looks skeptical. "Any idea when this will be?"

"Thirty years or so. You'll only be, what? Ninety-four."

She bats her eyes. Up close, her lashes are clearly false. Her lips purse to cover the smile, but she's pleased. She squeezes my arm until she realizes it, and then pulls away. I better say something more while I can. No telling who she'll be next.

"If you're worried about Steph, the way she acts—"

"Oh, I'm not concerned about Stephanie," Connie says. "In the first glance she saw just how far she could push me, and it was about that far." She holds up a finger and thumb pinched together until the nails meet. "What's to worry about her?"

"Well, you said that at her age, you were working for your living, so how—"

"I *was* working for my living at her age," Connie says. "I was lucky. You always need a little nudge to grow up. You don't do it on your own, and I had plenty of encouragement." She hesitates and then goes on. "I always have been lucky, and I still am. You want proof?"

She taps the back of my hand with a long red nail.

"If I wasn't luckier than I deserve, I wouldn't be sitting here with my grandson beside me. It doesn't get much better than this."

She turns away from me as if she hadn't spoken

and goes into a conversation with somebody on her other side. The red nail slips away from my hand.

The lights go out, and they bring in the baked Alaska, a preposterous dessert soaked in brandy and set on fire. Around here everything's a production number.

When we leave, I hold Connie's chair and give her my arm as we float out of the Magellan Room. She drags her fur along over the carpet behind her. Pretty stagy, and effective. She returns the headwaiter's bow, and we stop past the silver bowl of after-dinner mints. Connie likes a handful.

The Adriatica Room is already full of diamonds and old dinner jackets, but we've got a reserved table down front.

"How good can this show be without you in it?" I ask her.

"Better than you can imagine." She gives me a sly look.

I spot a threesome at a nearby table: a dad, a mom, and unless my eyes deceive me, Melanie Krebs. This near her parents she's slouched in the chair and turned away from them. She's in an upscale outfit, a lot of stuff on her eyes, and, as we know, a professional job done on her hair. Her leg's propped up, so I see she's wearing silver shoes, but flat.

I'm about to give up on Steph, though Connie isn't worried. Then I spot her, but only because I'm looking for her. Steph's coming down past the tiers of tables. I'm not sure what I think. At a distance, I wasn't sure it was Steph.

Her hair looks good and no junk on her face, except for a trace of lipstick. The dress gives her a year or so, an edge. It also gives her a figure. She even seems to have something of a waist. None of it is Steph's style. It's better than that. She looks both older and more like a little girl. She looks good, and when she hits our level, she kicks out, showing the shoes. She's staggering in them, but she's making it.

Across the aisle, Melanie's eyes are glued on her, but Steph doesn't seem to notice. Melanie's running a check on the dress, seeing it's cut lower behind. Her gaze drops to the two-inch silver heels, and she freezes. Then for some reason, Melanie turns on her mother, snarling.

Steph wobbles up to our table. Because she doesn't flop down, I'm up to help her into her chair. I don't get thanked for this, but we're making enormous strides. Connie doesn't react, which I'm beginning to see is her style. People keep handing her scraps of paper, and she's busy signing autographs. The stage lights come up, and Wilhelm's Melodiers blast out "The Best of Times Is Now," and it's show time.

The cruise director comes on to tell us what a great day at sea we've had. He introduces the comedian, who dies. In a room full of senior citizens, you don't make age jokes.

"You people want to know why they never give you ice water on this ship?"

Not particularly.

"Because you keep putting your teeth in the glass."

A disaster. Connie moans lightly and retreats behind her tinted shades. The comedian barely gets off with his skin and makes way for the baritone.

The show's theme is "Around the World in Eighty Days," something like that. The baritone begins with "Wonderful, Wonderful Copenhagen" because that's tomorrow's port. Then we get "Arrivederci, Roma," "A Foggy Day in London Town," two or three Irish ditties that mention Dublin, "Granada," and finally "I Left My Heart in San Francisco."

The audience is warmed up for the accordionist, who leaps onto the stage and does a selection of Italian street songs. They go over better than you can believe, and when they bring him back, it's "Lady of Spain."

It's time for the big number. The lights go purple, and the music goes French. From nowhere an electric Eiffel Tower appears.

The stage fills suddenly with four dancers wearing high-feathered headdresses and not much else. A feather here and there, a string of pearls, high-heeled shoes. That's about it. Otherwise, miles and miles of creamy flesh.

Connie nudges me. "Blink, boy. You'll ruin your eyesight."

The four feathered French dancers are all over the stage, and the hot lights are all over them. Three fall back, and a limelight hits the fourth, bathes her in bedazzling white. And she isn't even French. Under her feathered headdress her hair is blazing red. Her skin, a lot of it, is like—what? Seashells? Pearls?

It's Holly. My chin drops onto my bow tie. This goes farther than my fantasies. She's dancing with an imaginary partner, a . . . lover. The light's so strong that you're not sure what you're seeing, how much. I'm not sure how much I should be seeing, and I can't see enough. Then the light begins to flicker, and she's colorless, a figure in an old movie, showing more by showing less.

When her star turn is over, she falls in with the other dancers. They do a modified cancan, without skirts. The lights take us back to purple Paris. Everybody comes onstage again, and we have "The Last Time I Saw Paris." It's a big finish.

The applause brings them all back, but when the dancers take their bows, they're wearing short silky tops over their nothingness. It's over. I'm exhausted.

"Cha-cha-cha," Connie murmurs, "and she moonlights."

Chapter 7

According to the morning newsletter, today is

> *Copenhagen, capital of Denmark and throne of Europe's oldest royal dynasty. This "salty old queen of the sea" was founded as a fishing village in 1157 by Valdemar the First and is famous for its smørrebrød sandwiches. For group tours kindly apply to the cruise director's office or enjoy the day at leisure.*

After a day at sea, dry land's a novelty, so everybody's on deck. We're in the Sound, with Sweden on one side and Denmark on the other. We pass Hamlet's castle off our starboard side, and the Minoltas are clicking away.

I've had a bad night, and there's nothing worse

than insomnia in a windowless room. You're a hostage. I'm hung over this morning, though it's not the wine. It's something else. I'm not up for anything this morning, let alone a foreign port. But I cashed some money at the purser's desk, and it's kroners. Seven to the dollar. Figure that.

When we dock, I happen to notice from my lookout up on Promenade Deck that Steph's among the first ashore. She came down the gangplank with all the Krebses, but she and Melanie are ahead of the parents and moving out. It's possible that Steph has found her escape route.

Connie and I go ashore together. She's in a bigbrimmed hat that seems to form part of her wig, and regulation dark glasses. This could be Connie-thetourist, except how far will she get in those shoes? She comes up past my elbow, holding on.

A stretch Mercedes meets us at the pier. It seems that Connie was always a bigger star in the Danes' opinion than she was back home: a cult figure. A radio station has sent the limo. She's to tape an interview for them, and I happen to notice she can't wait.

A block or so past the ship, the limo slows so we can get a fleeting glimpse of the Little Mermaid, the famous statue out on a rock in the water. This isn't exactly sightseeing, but the limo's great.

"Do we get this treatment every time?"

Connie waves me away. "The next port's Russia. Enjoy this while you can."

We gun past four royal palaces in a square, and the next thing I know, I'm spending the day in an outer office, watching Connie being interviewed behind glass in a studio. They work in her old records. The songs blend, a minicourse. "Let Me Off Uptown." "Heartaches." Once with only a piano accompaniment, "You Made Me Love You."

I don't hear the interview. But they don't seem to be having a language barrier. Connie's coming alive behind her glasses. Her hands weave the past. Her smile's bigger, suitable for an album sleeve. The years roll off her as they do under the pink lights of her performance.

I'm looked after. While I wait, they bring me coffee and—what else? Danishes.

In the late afternoon, we're eating more of them in a sidewalk café. It's just Connie and me, but we're to meet the Krebses here later, along with cool Melanie and Steph.

"So how do you feel?" I ask Connie, about her day.

She overreacts with a sharp look. But then she sees I want her to admit she's been getting off on being a Danish superstar. She's not about to admit anything. "The question is, how do you feel?"

I survey the street scene: flowers, streetcars, the long row of white tables and bowing waiters—fantastic. According to my calculations, coffee and a pastry are ten bucks a crack here, and worth it. "Terrific."

"And yet," she says, "you walked the floor last night."

"You heard?"

"I knew."

She's playing old-and-wise with me, and I see you have to watch her or she'll do that.

"You were flying high at dinner last night," she recalls, "but something about the show took the wind out of your sails. I wonder if it was one of the dancers. Holly, for instance."

"Who?"

"You know who." Back in her throat she makes a little tick sound, the one Steph inherited.

I scoop up Danish crumbs with a casual gesture. "Look, I meet this girl, who's fantastic. Then when I . . . see her again, she's this completely remote . . . total woman, with feathers. Case closed. I'm fine. I may even find consolation someday, years down the line. It's been a . . . good learning experience for me."

Connie listens to this word flow and then says, "I don't know what a learning experience is, but does it mean you're going to moon around looking lovesick for the rest of the cruise?"

". . . No. But I think I'm a dance class dropout."

She sighs and seems to change the subject, which is fine with me. "In the old days, men were always falling for me. Then sometimes when they'd see me in front of the band in my war paint and cutting loose, they'd fade away. They couldn't handle it, and I always figured if they couldn't, they weren't worth my time."

"One could handle it," I say, not even meaning to.

Her eyebrows rise over her glasses.

"I don't know who. But if there wasn't one, I wouldn't be here."

She considers that. "You mean your grandfather. He was one of the other kind. He couldn't quite believe in me unless I *was* on the stage. But we were talking about you."

"We were?"

"You go on back to the dance class. You're safer with Holly than you know, and she doesn't have a thing to worry about with you. Getting turned down by her will teach you more than any little sophomore girl knows."

I clear my throat. "I'll be a junior . . . actually."

"Whatever," Connie says.

"Maybe I'll drop by the dance class again, just to brush up on my samba. We'll keep it on a businesslike basis."

"That's right," she says, hiding a smile. She can see right through me, though it's no big trip. She's chuckling down in her throat and dabbing a napkin under her glasses.

"Anyway," I say, "who says Holly's going to turn me down?"

I get lucky here, because I never hear the answer. We're suddenly surrounded by Krebses, and Steph.

They're all over us, at least Mr. and Mrs. Krebs are. It was their idea to round off our Denmark day together. And from the way Mr. Krebs is hovering around Connie, I'd say we have a fan on our hands. He came up, humming "What Is This Thing Called Love?" which is a pretty good sign. Connie seems willing to go along, and when the Krebses hear she has a condo on Singer Island, they get excited again because they're just down the road at West Palm Beach.

Mr. Krebs reminds me of Mr. Morthland, Florida style. Three-button linen sport coat, but pink. Tassels on his loafers, but white. Mrs. Krebs has a permanent tan and a slight accent that probably isn't West Palm Beach and a pair of good cheekbones Melanie will be lucky to inherit. Steph and Melanie are hanging back, especially Steph.

Daughters could learn a few things from mothers. Though I'm not about to try that concept on Steph. Mrs. Krebs looks as if she knows her way around the world, while Melanie looks as if she can't find her way out of the mall.

With her husband humming a backup, Mrs. Krebs says six or eight nice things to Connie. The last one being, "What a pleasure it must be to have your grandchildren with you this summer."

"It's more than that," Connie says, and even takes off her dark glasses for them.

Steph and Melanie shrink somewhat, trying not to be there, though we're all five knee to knee around the table. After a day in the stores, they're not quite clones, but close. They've bought matching everything, including the sweaters they're wearing. Steph's about half mellowed out. Copenhagen's a great shopping town, so Europe's looking up. She still hasn't broken herself of whispering around adults. While they mumble, Melanie keeps rolling her eyes my way. She may be precocious.

Mr. Krebs says we're going to round out the evening at Tivoli. Melanie and Steph put up some resistance until they learn it's the original theme park, like Disney World, but better.

It's a lot better. Colored lights twinkling through real trees, open-air theaters giving shows, Dixieland music drifting over European flower beds. Possibly the most beautiful spot in the world. We have dinner in a place on the grounds called Bel Terrass, Mr. Krebs's treat, and this guy seems to know that living well is the best revenge.

When he consults with Connie about the wine list, she just says, "The rule where I come from is: Never drink with the customers."

The Krebses think it's great show-business talk. It's also Connie keeping her distance, just the right amount.

I wish I knew how. After dinner, Melanie wants to go on one of the rides. This sounds a little young for her image, but she has a plan. There's one that's half roller coaster and half kiddies' ride. The cars look like a small vintage freight train. Suddenly I'm in the caboose with Melanie, though I don't remember getting here. This leaves Steph with Mr. Krebs in the coal car, while Mrs. Krebs and Connie watch from solid ground.

Melanie and I sit in this cockamamie caboose, waiting for it to go, and I'm fresh out of chat. What am I supposed to say? Ask her what grade she's in when I'm reasonably sure she's covering it up? *What's your major? What's your sign?* What am I doing here?

Our toy train begins to move and climb. We're over the twinkling lights and treetops. Copenhagen unfolds around us in the long evening: towers and spires, ribbons of traffic, ships at sea.

This would be great if Holly were sitting here instead of Melanie. And then it hits me: I am to Melanie what Holly is to me. I'm not Steph's geeky big brother. I'm Mr. Wonderful. Didn't Melanie first see me in a dinner jacket? It's all there in her big brown eyes. Is this the look I give Holly? Why do I have thoughts like these? At this particular point in time, Bates Morthland would be feeding Melanie a line, just for practice.

But she doesn't need conversation. Our tin train rolls over the crest and makes a tremendous first drop, all of twelve feet. Melanie screams and throws her arms around me. I'm being given the Heimlich maneuver by a love-crazed seventh grader, and her nails are really digging in.

At the end of the ride I see the nails are false and new, fresh today, and painted Steph-pink. "That was like *so neat*," Melanie says, climbing out of the caboose.

"Yeah," I say. "Wait till I tell them about it at school. I'll be a junior."

"I know." Melanie bats her big browns at me. "Which is *so neat.*"

We're at sea the next day, though some of us are more at sea than others. I seem to recall Connie encouraging me to go back to the dance class and Be Mature about Holly. But while I'm counting the minutes till the samba session and thinking about wimping out, Connie appears from nowhere. It's bouillon time, which means they're serving beef broth and crackers on the rear deck. A great day too: overcast sun and brisk breezes. We're entering the Baltic Sea.

"I have a little job for you." Connie's head is tied up in a turban. She's wearing her darkest glasses. And she's sounding too casual.

She takes me on a ten-minute walk deep into the ship, a level or two even lower than Coral Deck. We draw up in front of a closed door.

"It's Shep," she says. But I don't know Shep, and

she's looking annoyed, rattled. Another Connie. "Shepard Bailey, the piano player. He's my responsibility, more or less. I got them to take him on."

So we seem to be outside Shep's door. "Is he sick?" "He's drunk, and he's got to be sober enough to rehearse this afternoon, or . . . else." I can't see her face. Her forehead's almost against the door. "I poured a pot of coffee down him. I want you to take him to the sauna. I can't. There are separate saunas for men and women. Just let him . . . sweat it out."

"He can't make it on his own?"

"He'll think he can. But go with him."

She pushes open the door because she's told me enough. He's in there, Shep is. I haven't really noticed him up close before. A bald, gaunt-faced guy with a lot of broken veins in his nose. He's sitting on the end of his bed, dressed. His shirt's buttoned up to the collar, but no tie. He could use a shave. He squints up at us.

"Drew's going to go down to the sauna with you, Shep."

He's about to give her an argument, but doesn't. And so by eleven o'clock instead of being at Holly's samba lesson, I'm down in the health club sauna, trying to dry out a seventy-year-old drunk. This summer is just one thing after another.

I've never been in a sauna before. It's hot air all the way down to the lungs, and you have to find new methods of breathing. It smells funny, too, and I'm beginning to think it's Shep. I'm on the bench farthest from him, but the sauna's smaller than my cabin, and there's a distinct alcohol smell in here, maybe bourbon.

We're only wearing towels. I'm melting in mine. He looks terrible in his. What if it doesn't work right? What if he doesn't sober up, and I dissolve? They could find him in here later, alone with two towels.

He seems to think he's alone now, sitting up on the top bench with his face in his hands. He's pretty saggy, with blue veins in his legs. But his hands are different. Not exactly younger, but long and strong, a pianist's hands. For some reason it hurts to see them. Maybe because they're all he has left.

Once you start your major sweating, it gets easier. Your body adjusts, especially if you can keep the towel between you and the bench. I settle in and go into that same kind of daze I have in math class.

"You ever play the Blue Room of the Roosevelt, down in New Orleans? Seymour Weiss's place?"

This brings me around with a jerk. Shep's speaking through his hands. But he looks up and wipes the sweat off his brows. He works his shoulders, and they pop like corn. "No, of course not. You're too young."

"And no musical abilities either," I say.

"You're better off." He grins a little. "But you'll have to work for a living."

He shifts around on the slats. "I played them all,

100

the big places and the not so big places, then the cocktail lounges, and finally the toilets.

"Listen, I drank myself out of some of the best bands in the business. Ever hear of Ted Weems? Wayne King? Jan Garber? Then one day they weren't even there. The year after the war was over, eight of the big ones broke up." He snaps his fingers at how fast they went.

"Why?"

"Who knows? The war was over. People went home. Then television kept them at home. And the singers. They killed the bands as quick as anything else. They started working farther in front until you couldn't tell which band it was. Sinatra? Rosemary Clooney?"

"Connie?" I say.

"Not Connie." He looks up, rubs his hands down his arms the way you have to do in a sauna. "No, with Connie the band came first, last, and always. She was on the band bus as long as there was a band bus. She never really wanted anything else." He suddenly looks—not sober, but younger, around the eyes.

"You should have been there in the old days. She was something. She wasn't even that good. She was great. You take some of the best-looking women in the business, some of the best singers—they didn't want to follow her. I hadn't seen her in years, before now. I hadn't seen anybody in years."

He starts to get up, cracks his bald head on the low

ceiling, and then eases down to plant a foot on the floor, carefully. He's standing up, with a good grip on the towel. He's making it, but he'd be sweating anywhere.

"You've got these moments in life when you don't know which you need most, a drink or the job. I have 'em all the time."

He looks for the door, finds it. I make a little move.

"It's okay." He waves at me. "Today I need the job." He shoves the door open. "What'd you say your name was?"

"Drew. Drew Wingate."

Shep works his shoulders. "Sounds like a law firm." Then he shuffles out, leaving big footprints.

I stay awhile longer, but the bourbon smell doesn't go away. I happen to remember a good-sized Jacuzzi outside, which sounds like the next step.

Taking a long shower, I turn it up gradually to cold-as-I-can-stand-it. This has a shriveling effect, but it stops the sweating, cold. Then I push through a couple of doors to the Jacuzzi room, which is empty except for a pair of plastic palm trees.

Dropping my towel, I slip into the swirling waters. It's great. I'm in this ship cutting through the Baltic Sea, but I'm down deep in it, bobbing in this private sea of my own. Worlds within worlds. I go back into my daze.

A door opens somewhere, and through slitted eyes I see a vision. It could be sculpture, except it's wearing a one-piece swimsuit. The arms, alabaster, are up, with hands pushing hair under a bathing cap. Fiery red hair.

It's Holly. Eight hundred people on this ship, and it's Holly. I've been floating dangerously near the surface, but my feet fight down through the currents to find the bottom. Still, I'm not completely convinced I'm naked. I'm too disoriented for that. Isn't this the men's Jacuzzi? My head whirls, pounds. It's like finals. Then it comes to me. Why didn't somebody tell me? Why am I always the last to know? There's one Jacuzzi for both sexes, situated between the men's department and the . . .

Holly spots me. She rests her hands on her fleshless hips. "And where was my star pupil for the samba session?" she wants to know. I see her dancer's legs all the way up. I've seen more of her, in the show. This is better, but I can't concentrate. I think of covering myself up, or is the swirling water doing it? I pray for whitecaps.

"How much of that have you had?" Holly asks, concerned. "Your face is red as beetroot."

I try to answer but my mouth's filling with whirled hot water. Because I've decided to drown myself. I even let the waters close over my head, but I bob back. Suicide in a Jacuzzi could take more time than I have.

She's nearer now, testing the water with a toe. My mind's backpedaling, my tongue's paralyzed. I can feel my nakedness all the way down. I'm not Melanie's Mr. Wonderful anymore. I'm naked as a jaybird in a coed health club. I'm not even legal. And any minute now Holly's going to be in this crock pot with me. She slips in and settles against the opposite side, stretches her graceful arms out along the top of the tub. "Heaven," she says, sinking neck deep. "The dance class was particularly grueling. We were short a man."

I stare at her, trying to see how much of the human body you can identify below water level. Her eyes are nearly shut, though she knows I'm staring. But does she know why? Her top half is clearly visible, though wavery and green. Farther down, I'm not sure what I'm seeing.

"Nice day in Copenhagen?" she asks.

"F-f-fine."

"I didn't get ashore at all. We're working up some new routines and had to walk through them."

I blow a few bubbles, trying to keep this water in motion. I don't have time for conversation, or the attention span. It hits me how witty I was going to be the next time Holly and I met. Kicked back but witty. Mature, maybe a little mysterious. It hits me hard. My eyes begin to sting at the unfairness of everything. I'm regressing to Steph. I'd bang a door if I could. I glance at the door to the men's sauna and wonder how I can get there without taking my body. My towel's way out of reach. Figures.

104

"It's curious," Holly remarks. "They say the Jacuzzi is conducive to conversation, but I seem to be carrying the entire burden."

I manage a smile. Though it must look more like a silent scream because her eyes widen. "I say, I really think you've had enough."

I say I haven't. I say I'm staying in here till I'm ready to be sliced and served at Roy Rogers. But I don't say anything out loud. I could confess, of course, and we could both have a big laugh. It's the mature way out of this. On the other hand, I won't be sixteen till next week, and maturity's still a bit out of reach. But I have to say something.

"Cope?" I say, "nhagen?"

"I beg your pardon?"

"Nice day in Copenhagen? Did you have one?"

She sighs. "I thought we'd covered that."

Covered. What did she mean by that?

Then a sudden sound blasts through the area, echoing. Like the crack of doom, and I wish it was. Two longs and a short . . . deafening. I leap, but not too high. "What is it?" I say, near the end of my rope. "What's happening?"

"Out we go," Holly says, bobbing up. "It's door drill. Just an exercise. They'll be closing all the water-tight doors in the ship to make sure they're working. But we'll have to get out of the health club. There's just time if we hurry. You can come along just as you are."

That's what you think, lady.

Holly's edged up onto the tiles, swooping her legs out of the water. She's glancing back at me, and I can read it in her eyes. She thinks I'm retarded.

Panic's a terrible thing. It steers you wrong every time. I could probably wait her out. Timing is everything, but I'm too trapped to think straight.

Holly's on her feet, turned away from me. She's pulling off her bathing cap, distracted. I see my chance. I can vault out of the Jacuzzi behind her back, head for the men's door by way of my towel, and be home free. I can be a Road Runner cartoon.

With a mighty effort I throw a leg out of the water, across my body, and snag a hold on the edge of the tub with my knee. I'm up, out of the water, except my knee slips off. I'm back in, face down in foam, mooning the world.

I'm up again, though, and out of the Jacuzzi, with hands and knees planted on the tile floor. Then I'm standing, then I'm down on a slick spot, then I'm up and running. My towel's miles away. How did it get so far? Scooping it up in a death grip, I plunge to the door. I never think to wrap the towel around me. I'm nearly gone, but I know she's turned to watch. Who wouldn't? I sounded like a crazed whale in the water, and it's taken me an hour and a half to run ten feet. I'm through the door, but I feel her eyes, burning, and I'm sure I hear her: stifled shrieks of British laughter.

Chapter 8

Leningrad, USSR, formerly Petrograd and founded as St. Petersburg in 1703. Czar Peter the Great heaped riches upon his capital as Russia's Window on the West, rising from the marshes of the Neva River. Only group tours permitted ashore. Passengers must apply to the cruise director, as we have a limited number of bus seats left.

After two days of not going to the dance class, I could use a new port. I'm keeping clear of the health club, the sun deck. I don't go places where you take your clothes off, any of them. I eat and go to the bingo sessions and lose myself in crowds. A little younger, and I'd be sulking. Steph is, ever since Copenhagen.

"Mr. and Mrs. Krebs only like Connie, and Melanie

only likes you. I'm so betrayed I can't believe it. It's just like at home. Nobody thinks about me."

But an hour later I catch Steph and Melanie together, checking out times for an Eddie Murphy movie in the ship theater.

This means they both miss the lecture in La Panoramique we're all encouraged to attend the afternoon before Leningrad. We're about to penetrate the Iron Curtain, and these people have a lot of rules. The currency is rubles, and we have to declare how many we're taking into the country, but we're not supposed to take any in. It's a little confusing.

We won't be wandering around Leningrad on our own. You sign up for an eighty-five-dollar bus tour, and you stick with it. We'll be allowed to take pictures, but not of the dock, military posts, anybody in uniform, or people lined up in front of stores. Fun city.

With some time on my hands, I go to the purser and buy a postcard with Lenin on it and pen a message to an old friend.

Bates, my man,

Here on the high seas I met a girl and implemented my program. It looked good for a few moonlit nights, but didn't work out. So I'm defecting. Best of luck in your future endeavors, if any.

Drew

I even address it. Then I take another look at Lenin, decide maybe this isn't joke time, and tear up the card. I'm a lousy correspondent anyway.

We wake up already docked, and everybody's on deck, gazing down at a long covered pier. Here we are in Russia, and it could use a coat of paint.

Connie appears, in shades and turban. Evidently she isn't going to waste a wig on the Russians. We haven't seen much of her the past couple of days. She admits to a touch of sea sickness and hasn't turned up for bingo, which she loves. But here she is.

"I wouldn't miss it," she says, hooking my arm. I figure she means the bus tour.

We're marched along a crumbling pier past a platoon of Russian soldiers, about my age, with guns. Then there's a lot of nonsense in the customs shed about swapping our real passports for temporary Russian ones. These people definitely have an attitude problem. We stand with mirrors behind us to make sure we aren't smuggling CIA personnel in our back pockets. With my luck, there'll be a strip search.

Outside by the buses, Connie's spotting for the Krebses and Steph. We manage to be the last two aboard their bus. Steph and Melanie are sharing a seat and an image: similar Guess? tops, matching Levi's, Reeboks, fingernails. Connie and I take the only two empties at the back, where she settles in, swinging her heels and looking unusually alert.

Boris is our bus driver. But I don't catch our Intourist guide's name. She's no smiler and doesn't seem too happy at being outnumbered by Americans. She gives us a rundown on Leningrad, but we're already moving through the streets, and it speaks for itself.

A gray, tired city with a fantastic view here and there. A bridge like iron cobwebs over a canal. A gold dome against the hot blue sky. Spooky, depressing, beautiful—I don't know. It's ninety degrees in the bus and maybe hotter outside, and yet the place feels like autumn, quiet and dusty and not a lot of people around, considering there are four million of them. It also feels like Sunday, and maybe it is. I'm beginning to lose track of time on this trip.

We stop at a park the size of a traffic island and take pictures. Across the Neva River is the Winter Palace. In another direction is the old fortress. Back on the bus we walk by where Mrs. Krebs is sitting. She glances up but doesn't seem to see us. Her hands are clenched in her lap. Mr. Krebs doesn't even look up. I don't think they got off the bus.

We tour the city, or at least drive around, and then they take us to the Hotel Pribaltiiskaya, a mammoth place at the edge of town. Hundreds of us sit down to lunch in the same dining room, with a full orchestra playing old Russian tunes.

We're at a big table with the Krebses, but Mrs. Krebs isn't eating anything, and Mr. Krebs isn't saying much, even to Connie. We're not exactly in the

right town for light conversation anyway. But something really heavy seems to be hanging over the
Krebses. In front of us is a monster meal with vodka
—we've been warned about the water. A lot of food,
weird and heavy, but good.

"I don't eat any of this stuff, whatever it is," Steph
announces. But she's willing to sample the black-
berry jam. She piles it on a cracker and learns too late
that it's caviar: salty black fish-eggs in glue. Her eyes
bulge. She gags.

"Gross me out," she says to Melanie in a whisper
they can hear in the Kremlin. "Why are we even
here?"

But Melanie looks away. She doesn't even have
eyes for me.

In the afternoon we're bused to the Hermitage,
the art collection in the Winter Palace. Before they
let us inside, we have to wait in an incredibly impressive square, and by now, Steph's about had it. In the
square, mysterious figures keep coming up to her,
wanting to buy her Levi's straight off her body. After
the Hermitage, we have one more stop, another park
for pictures, with a big cathedral in the distance and
benches in the shade along the walks.

An old lady's sitting at the end of one of the
benches. I wouldn't have noticed her. We're nowhere near her, but Connie's watching the Krebses
. . . every move. Steph's fallen back with us.

Mrs. Krebs, holding Melanie's hand, is walking toward the old lady. Their eyes are meeting, but at the last moment the woman on the bench looks aside. But her arms are out now, gathering and anxious. Mrs. Krebs—classy Mrs. Krebs all dressed up—drops to her knee, and her arms circle the old lady's waist. Then the old lady reaches out and runs her hand over Melanie's face. Melanie holds back, but then moves in closer. If there are any words, we can't hear them. Mr. Krebs stands back, blinking in the sun.

And still I don't begin to understand. Neither does Steph, quiet beside me. Connie's watching these people, knowing what it means, and what it means to them.

Behind us, the bus is boarding, and Boris is hitting the horn. Tour-groupers melt out of the park. So it's over that quick, quicker than telling about it. Connie turns away, like she's remembered not to stare. Steph and I follow, so we don't see the Krebses leaving the bench with the woman on it. They're the last three back on the bus. And there in the distance, hazy in the heat, an old lady's sitting on a park bench.

The day never gets dark. The Russians call them "white nights" when summer evening lingers on till dawn. We sail late, with recorded Red Army march music blasting out of a loudspeaker on shore. And the city's still suspended between silver sky and silver water.

Connie's too tired for dinner in the Magellan Room. She plans a picnic for us in her cabin, hers and Steph's. There's not an inch to spare in here, but it's our own safe little world, after Russia.

Steph and I are lined up on one of the beds, and Connie's in the chair by her dressing table. In her turban and wrapper, she gives the place a real backstage feel. Her wedding picture is propped up behind her, dusty with face powder. All we need is light bulbs around the mirror, and this could be behind the scenes at the old Stardust Ballroom somewhere.

Stavros thinks the picnic idea is great. He arrives with trays up and down his arms: cold cuts, salads, feta cheese, desserts, more than we'd order in the Magellan Room. He comes back with a champagne cooler full of Poopsie: the works.

Connie isn't hungry. She wants to talk about the day. She'd known what was happening. Mrs. Krebs had told her in Copenhagen, when we were on the ride at Tivoli. Mrs. Krebs is—was a Russian. They let her out of the country, and she became an American citizen. She married Mr. Krebs, and they had Melanie.

"Mrs. Krebs went through all the paperwork to get her mother out and bring her to Florida," Connie says, "but the Russians wouldn't let her go. Finally, her mother was too old to make the change. And still, she'd never seen her granddaughter."

"Melanie," Steph murmurs.

"And the family was never permitted to visit Russia. The only way was a cruise. You can take a day's tour of Leningrad without having a visa. This is the third year they've made the trip, but the first time they were able to meet the grandmother."

I look up at that, not following it.

"She lives in Moscow, not Leningrad. The first year when she was coming to meet her family, the authorities took her off the train. The second year, they held her in the train station in Leningrad until the ship sailed. This year it worked, for some reason. Mrs. Krebs was awfully afraid it wouldn't."

"I don't get it," I say. "If the Krebses don't even apply for visas, how could the Russians know the grandmother was coming to Leningrad to meet them?"

"Mrs. Krebs would have written to her mother," Connie says, "and the mail would have been opened and read."

It reminds me of something. That book we did in ninth grade . . . *1984.* I thought it was supposed to be about the future, not now. I thought we had a little leeway.

Connie watches me through her at-home glasses. They're bifocals, untinted. Behind them, her eyelashes are like big black flowers.

"It's not fair," Steph says, one of her oldest sayings. But it has new meaning now, and maybe she realizes.

The three of us sit there, together by ourselves. You

114

can hear the steady throb of the ship, and usually you only notice it in bed at night. Steph picks all the crumbs off her lap and makes a pile of them. She glances at the door.

I thought I was the only one who can see Steph thinking, but Connie says, "I think you ought to leave Melanie with her parents tonight. Let them be family."

It lets us be family, too, but Connie doesn't say so. Maybe she doesn't think of it. Maybe she doesn't dare. But this is the first moment that calling her Connie doesn't seem accurate enough. She's our grandmother, and I'm not sure how we ever got along without her.

We're family here, and though it isn't exactly Steph's favorite word, her eyes dart away from the door, and she settles back on her elbows. Maybe she even wants to stay with us, but she also wants the last word. It's one of her rules.

"If I'm going to hang around here, we've got to clean up this pigpen." Steph purses her lips. Every time I look at her, I see one more trait she's inherited from Connie. Or is she picking them up? "Ring for Stavros to take away all these dishes and that ice bucket thing. I've got Poopsie coming out of my ears."

Connie bats big lashes at me, and rings.

Before Stavros gets here, Steph's off the bed and down on the floor, pulling out Connie's shoes from everywhere and lining them up in the closet. "I have never seen anybody as messy as you are, Connie," Steph says, down on all fours. "Honestly."

This blows me out of the water. Steph's the messiest person I've ever seen. But I check around, and all the litter looks like Connie's. Maybe she is messier. She just sits there, looking innocent.

"And another thing," Steph says from the floor. "I wish you'd find someplace to keep those wigs of yours besides out in the open where everybody can see. It's like that movie about the man with his head chopped off, and he keeps it in a pan."

Connie cocks her little turbaned head. I don't think she's seen this movie. But she's busy now, arranging all our dirty plates with her own on the bottom so Stavros won't know she didn't clean up her plate.

116

Chapter 9

Helsinki, capital of Finland and 143 nautical miles from Leningrad, is a flower-bedecked city of smiles and Sibelius. This "Daughter of the Baltic" reveres nature, neutrality, and the best in modern design. Docking approximately 10:30 A.M.

Personally, I can't wait. We're back to breathing free air, and my day starts with an invitation under the door. Connie gets them all the time, invitations to cocktail parties in suites up on Mykonos Deck, the high-rent district. But she doesn't drink with the customers, and my invitation's from Holly.

She's invited me to lunch in Helsinki. I'm willing to write her off as a lost cause, and she's willing to invite me to lunch in the dining room of Stockmann's, whatever that is. A miracle.

117

Something about Leningrad has reordered my priorities, and I've got to stop being so petty and self-conscious. It's like going through life wondering if your fly is open. So okay, the last time Holly saw me, I was skinny-dipping by mistake. It could happen to anybody, and she only saw me going the other way. There's still a little mystery left, so to speak.

Stavros brings me a room-service breakfast, and I can reread my invitation in privacy. Connie, in her wrapper, pops by and catches me smelling the paper in case it's perfumed. Either she can read it with X-ray vision, or she already knows. She already knows.

She says she'd invite herself along, which freezes my blood, but Gala Night's coming up, and she has to go over her charts. "I'll pass up Helsinki."

"You can catch it next time around," I say.

She settles on my bed, already made by superhuman Stavros. "No, this is the last time. And I've had to turn down Stephanie. She wanted me to join her and Melanie. They've heard of a place here with Chicago pizza."

Steph? Inviting Connie to lunch? Before this trip, Steph couldn't tell one adult from another, and she sure never took one to lunch. She never looked higher than high school. But I've got more pressing issues. Connie's behind me, and our eye contact is via the mirror.

"Look, a major glamour figure's lunching me in a

118

great European capital. What am I supposed to wear?"

Connie thinks. "That light-blue blazer, a golf shirt, your white pants, deck shoes."

When you ask Connie, you have to watch her, or she'll give you an answer. "Nautical," she says, "but nice." She's at my door, but lingering. "Have fun," she says.

"But don't get my hopes up?"

"From what I heard Holly telling around," Connie says, wide eyed, "you might get more than you bargained for." Then she vanishes.

I'm the first one ashore in Fabulous Finland. They don't even want to see your passport. They just wave you into their country. It's blue and green, sunwashed. Long evergreen fingers reach out into a sea gleaming like chrome. The choppy harbor's full of sails, and every island in it is capped with a little peaked-roof yacht club. There's a big open market selling crafts and vegetables and morning coffee, which I have.

Fishermen sell their catches off boats tied up at the market wharf. Across the way, in a park called the Esplanadi, a statue of a girl is being coy in an explosion of flowers. Not a bad town.

Stockmann's turns out to be the major department store, full of my fellow passengers. I kill time with some shopping, five Finnmarks to the dollar. Since timing is everything, I show up in the dining room on the dot. It's not what I pictured. Like the Adriatica Room, it's another big space with tables on tiers, nightclub style. And it's packed. But Holly stands at a table down front and puts up her hand.

Her red hair glints, and my heart heaves. I start toward her, concentrating on not falling down or knocking trays out of waiters' hands, or doing anything extra.

"Here we are, darling," she says, reaching out to take me in. Which is pretty thoughtful of her because everybody looks up to see I'm this stud—studlet—who's having lunch with the best-looking woman in the room.

Except it's a table for five. I feel a slight puncture in my poise. Four of the best-looking women in the room are sitting around it, smiling up at me. The scene's so close to a three-dimensional fantasy that I don't know whether to burst into tears or applause.

We haven't exactly met, but I've seen a lot of all of them. They're the French dancers from the ship, the full foursome, and not a Frenchwoman among them.

"Helga," Holly says, doing the introductions, "from Düsseldorf, Jean from Inverness, and Sandi from . . . somewhere peculiar. Where, Sandi?"

"Omaha," bouncy Sandi says, lighting up this end of the room with her smile. The cat's got my tongue.

I don't even get to sit next to Holly, and did she arrange that? This isn't how I had it figured at all. But I've got a great view of her. Her seashell skin's trans-

120

lucent in this light, and her eyes are emeralds. I wonder how she does it. And her profile. I haven't gotten around to memorizing her profile, but then I've been pretty busy. I'm between Jean and Sandi, and I've got to start somewhere. This is bound to be my biggest date in high school. Jean's darkish with a prominent chest. I remember her thighs from the show.

"So, tell me . . . Jean, what part of England is Inverness in?" I ask her.

"Och, you puir knothead. I'm from Scotland. Dinna anyone ever tell you the difference?"

". . . Ah . . ."

"I'm nothing like the English." She inhales deeply and rolls hazel eyes at me. "An English girl is all right for a night," says Jean, "but a Scotswoman is good for a lifetime."

"A night in Scotland is *like* a lifetime," Holly remarks, and they're off and running, except for Helga, who doesn't get punch lines. I find myself settling in, and the waiter wonders how I've pulled this off.

I even decide to try with my other lunch partner. "So tell me, Sandi, are you seeing anybody regularly?"

"Just my dentist," says Sandi, blinding me with a smile.

Anyway, the meal's great, though four of us are watching our figures, and one of us is watching their figures. We start off with *savustettua poronlihaa,* which I find out too late is cold smoked reindeer.

When Sandi finds out, her rosy lips droop at the corners. "Oh, bummer," she says, "it's like eating Rudolph." And Helga really doesn't follow this.

For the main course we have *karhu,* which I find out too late is bear. "Poor Paddington," Holly murmurs, shooting Sandi an innocent look.

Berries for dessert, called *lakka,* which look safe and taste fine. Except I keep inhaling these gusts of perfume around me, the same scent that hangs over the shop on the ship. Maybe they get it wholesale.

I'm finishing my *lakka* alone, just me and a waiting waiter. My fantastic foursome have risen up in a body and scampered off together, ticking away across the stage area in eight high heels. I guess they do that. They retire to the powder room and tell secrets, or something.

Now a tall Finnish woman is dragging a microphone onstage, and all the lunchers scrape their chairs around to face her. Why am I always the last to know? The woman gives a long pitch in Finnish, not a language you can pick up on your noon hour.

A music tape starts to roll, and from a secret door Holly floats out, with a spotlight on her. She's wearing a snow-white fur coat with turned-up collar, and her red hair's swirling above it. Her dancer's feet carry her to center stage, where she turns, sweeps around. The light winks on her smile. Her knee peeps through the opening of the coat. She extends one arm to somebody in the front row, who feels her

fur sleeve. She heads for my table, and sits down.
Now Jean's coming on, in mink.

What we have here is a—what? A fashion show.
"We do it every time we're in Helsinki. Aren't they
sweet to ask us?" Holly says to me, and now Jean's
made her turn and settles in beside me, and Helga's
coming on, in silver fox. Actually, Helga's the best-
looking one of the bunch, blond of course, and sort of
severe. Dynamite.

Then I realize what I'm thinking. How can Helga
be the best looking when Holly's the love of my life?
Can it be? Am I not in love with Holly? Am I in love
with all women? My face goes hot with sudden
awareness and the usual embarrassment.

Sandi's coming on now, looking great, in a fun fur
for the slopes, with a hood. Her face is grinning out,
perky: half Vanna White and half snow-bunny and all
American. She gives the crowd a big wink.

Holly's watching me, and as we know, she reads
minds. Her hand comes across the table to mine. I
take time off from Sandi to notice Holly's wrist, deli-
cate against the turned-back furry sleeve. She's
reaching between Helga and Jean, but their eyes are
on Sandi, who's extending her spotlight time.

Holly's hand closes over mine, and squeezes. "It's
fine," she says—quiet, but I hear her. "You can love
us all. I'd like a little more, though. Shall we always
be friends?"

So yes, I've been set up, and yes, it's fine. And yes, I

want to be Holly's friend. It isn't settling for anything. Seems to me Helga and Jean on either side of me are snuggling nearer. And now we're swept up in applause for Sandi, adding to it.

When she joins us, it's like a fur farm. I'm drowning in pelts. They're up again, taking their bows, grouping themselves to show the coats together, then dashing off.

It's mainly a fur show. They all come on again in three more changes, and a voice-over gives prices. But it's already dawned on me this is a business day, not a date. I'm into the swing of it now, mellowing nicely, until Holly comes on one last time. When the spotlight hits her, she rocks the room.

She's wearing a swimsuit, if you can call it that, about two Finnmarks' worth of material, top and bottom. You can't even see the color of it. There isn't enough there. One of the waiters drops a tray with an almighty crash. Then Jean comes on in a couple of bandanas, and I've already got my eyes peeled for Helga. She's no disappointment. Then Sandi, in about three polka dots, looking like the world's most dangerous sorority girl.

Now they're back at the table, all around me, throwing my biorhythms for a loop. Their naked legs disappear under the tablecloth. I shouldn't stare, but where else can I look? In every direction it's curves and cleavage and the occasional tiny mole.

Then the photographer who's been shooting onstage turns on our table. The world goes black from his flash, and I'm there in his camera: me in my blazer and golf shirt with four nearly naked beauties in a European capital. What wouldn't I give for a blowup of this picture—the size of my locker? For proof?

I can't account for the rest of the afternoon. The pay my fine furry foursome gets for being Stockmann models is twenty percent off on all purchases, so all four of them scatter for an afternoon of heavy-duty shopping.

I wander the streets of Helsinki, lightly stunned. The transition from Holly to a world full of Hollys makes me wonder if maybe a few of them are still in high school, say junior year. What I ought to do is work up my conversational skills. How many times do you want to be called puir knothead?

When I get back to the ship, passengers are beginning to stream up the gangplank, weighted down like bag people with their purchases. It's evening, but still full daylight, and I stroll around the ship, which feels like home by now.

In La Panoramique slow-dancing couples move to the strains of the three-piece string group. The cocktail buffet is setting up on the Promenade Deck. In El Morocco they're taking the covers off the blackjack tables, ready to play as soon as we sail. Then a hand grasps my shoulder.

Turning, I'm face-to-face with Holly. My old fantasies gang up on me again, and she's even panting. But there's a difference in her face. She's almost not the same girl . . . woman.

"I've been right over the ship looking for you." That, too, fuels my fantasies, and now she's dragging me away. "Don't dawdle, for heaven's sake."

We're out of the ship, down the gangplank, and there aren't many people around now. Holly hasn't got time to talk, and she's having trouble with her heels on the cobblestones.

"Why didn't I change into proper shoes?" she says, and still I don't know why we've jumped ship.

We're away from the docks and onto the streets of Helsinki, and I'm trying to match her, stride for stride. She's coming out with a couple of curses, too, half under her breath. They seem to be aimed at somebody called Leo.

"Who's Leo?"

"He's the degenerate on drums," she says, pretty fierce.

I try to picture the guy behind the drums with the Melodiers.

"He came back to the ship high as a kite—wrecked and running his mouth. He'd spent the whole day in some sewer of a bar with—there it is."

We're at an intersection, and Holly sees the sign for a bar down the block. I don't try asking her anything else. She's conserving her breath, cursing her shoes and Leo. She tucks a strand of hair behind her ear, and now we're pushing through the door of the bar.

It's dark inside, beery, and mainly empty except for a bartender who looks like he doesn't want to be involved. A piano's in the corner, and somebody's slumped over it, asleep on the keys. Holly makes right for him, and I see it's Shep. He's drunk, possibly dead drunk, and—

"Out of a job unless we get him back to the ship." Holly grips her own wrist, covering the face of her watch because she doesn't even want to know how close we are to sailing time. "I couldn't have managed him on my own."

I get on his other side to see if I can lift him under the arms. He's deadweight, but his hands come up, and his long fingers work over the keys, almost finding a melody.

Holly turns on the bartender. "You might at least have the decency to call us a cab *at once*." But he turns up his hands to let us know he speaks no English.

I'm edging Shep along to the end of the piano bench, but it looks hopeless. I remember him in the sauna, his head banging the ceiling. He's a big old guy. He keeps slipping away, and I get handsful of his coat.

"Blind and deaf with drink," Holly says, pretty disgusted, but doing what she can.

"Shep, stand up," I say loud in his ear. He throws a

127

leg around the end of the bench. His eyes are open, but Holly's right. He's not seeing anything. Trying, though. He eases up, knees shaky, and Holly gets on his other side. He's sagging there between us, but I feel his hand come up and take hold of my shoulder. It's pitiful, and makes me want to try harder for him. Still, I don't think we're going to get him there.

"Holly, maybe he just doesn't want to go."

Her eyes snap, even in this dim light. "That has nothing to do with it."

We're getting him to the door when the bartender speaks, in perfect English. "He has a bar bill."

Holly freezes. She plunges her hand down in the purse hanging from her free shoulder, grabs a handful of coins of all nations, and with a mighty sweep flings them at the bartender. They ping off the mirror, roll everywhere. If it wasn't too late to love her, I'd love her now.

We never find a cab, but he does better in the open air, and I won't let go if Holly won't. Finally, we're in sight of the ship, sensationally big and still at anchor. I'd pictured it halfway down the bay by now. We're not making good time over the cobblestones, but Holly's yelling to the distant figures getting ready to pull up the gangplank. The ship's horn roars with a sound that blasts the world.

We get him up the gangplank, another project. On board, he tries to do without us. There are people around, officers in gold braid, and so Holly smiles. It's an artificial smile, and probably not enough to take every eye off Shep.

We can't get him down all the stairs to his deck, so we wait for the elevator. When the doors open, Connie's inside. She's in one of her pantsuits and her number-three wig. In a glance at us, she sees it all. When she looks at Shep, her little chin comes up.

She puts out her hands to him, coaxing almost. It's ridiculous. She's half his size. If he fell . . . but he doesn't. He staggers, but makes it into the elevator. I put my hand out to keep the door from closing, but Connie waves me away.

"You've both done enough," she says. "It's my responsibility."

The doors close, and Holly and I are alone out in this lobby. It's almost as if nothing has happened. But Holly's watching me. We're both just there, a little footsore in deep carpeting. The floor wobbles when the ship edges away from the pier.

"Go down there and be with them."

I hardly hear her. She turns, but looks back because I haven't moved.

"She'll take him to her cabin, in case they look for him in his own." When she walks away, she sways only as much as the ship does. I start down the flights to Coral Deck.

Connie's door is open a crack. She's managed to get him here and down on the bed. He's out, or nearly, and she's standing over him, running her hand over her forehead. I don't know if she wants me here, but I push in, and she only looks up. When I start taking off Shep's shoes, she settles into her chair.

"You and Holly found him?"

"She knew where he was. We went to get him. He was in—"

"I can imagine."

I've got his shoes off, but he's wearing a tie that's strangling him. While I'm working on him, trying to keep out of range of his breath, he turns over. But I get his collar loose and whip off the tie. It's a mess: polka-dot with stains, even a little damp. I drop it into the wastebasket and can't think of anything else to do. He's breathing so loud, it's almost a relief. I stand back.

"Will he be all right?" I ask Connie.

"No, of course he won't. His liver's shot. He doesn't eat his meals. I should have left him where he was." She balls up her little fist and smacks the tabletop. "I was a fool."

She's fragile—and fierce, bunched in the chair, not looking over at him, trying to wall him out of her mind. She glances at the picture on her dressing table.

"Holly knows," she says. "I never told, but she put two and two together."

"Knows what, Connie?"

She's still looking at the picture.

130

"Shep and I . . . go way back." Connie brings up a sigh, impatient with me. "He's your grandfather."

We're suspended there. I am. I don't seem to know where I am, or who. Connie's not meeting my eye. She's looking at the door behind me.

"And so you see, I've been a fool about that guy more than once."

From here I can't quite see the wedding picture, of Connie and . . . Shep in his army uniform. I know his service cap comes to a sharp point over his forehead. His uniform buttons are Brassoed. A big, good-looking guy with a grin, as I remember. Mom said once he'd been a soldier. I guess I didn't think of him as anything else. I guess I have a pretty simplified view of the past.

"He doesn't know." Her mouth turns down at how meaningless this all is. "He didn't even know about your mother. And he wouldn't have any idea who you two are. He never cared about anything like that."

The ship creaks because we're in open water. The paneling on the walls wheezes, and the door behind me seems to sway.

"We got married on the spur of the moment, one night after a show." Connie's voice is forty-five years back. "People did then. Wartime. He was going overseas. But it wasn't based on anything. It was over before the war was. People used to get their divorces in Reno. I got mine. By June of forty-five, I was on the

Astor Roof, singing with Harry James and trying not to look pregnant. On the belt of my dress I pinned a spray of gardenias the size of a catcher's mitt."

She's still gazing at the picture, and so she waves it away in that hand gesture she has. Still, she won't look at me, only past me. "We were better off apart."

"Do you still . . . love him?"

She doesn't bother much with that. "I never did, not really. And I'm glad now." She looks over toward him. There's a hole in his sock, and she doesn't look higher than that.

"Then why bring him back, Connie?"

But somebody's pushing me aside, from behind. I jump a foot. I thought we were alone in this ocean. It's Steph, and she's heard. She's been standing in the door, and Connie's been talking to her, too, maybe mostly to her. Steph moves in on us.

She looks past the figure on one bed and drops her shopping bags down on the other. She's bought out the town in—where were we? Helsinki.

It's Steph in another new top, her old Reeboks, and the Levi's the Russians never got off her. Her hands are on her hips, with her big fingernails splayed out all over her thighs.

"Well, Connie, we can't leave him here," she says. "He can't be a what-do-you-call-it? A stowaway. And he can't work. Forget that, Connie, right?"

Connie sits up straighter. If she was anywhere near giving up, Steph has brought her back, and me too.

"He ought to be in the ship's hospital where they can look after him," I say.

Connie settles back, older and easier. Her grandchildren take over, and she looks relieved. A little guilty, but relieved.

We get busy, especially Steph, who's bustling around. We're bouncing off each other in this place, and Steph rings for Stavros. Before she starts ordering me around, I decide to go down to Shep's cabin for the things he'll need in the hospital. I'm beginning to suspect Steph of organizational abilities.

But Connie snaps her fingers, the way she does when she's rehearsing the band.

When we turn to her, she says, "Remember. I want you both to remember. He wasn't always a drunken bum. He could play some fine piano."

Chapter 10

~~~~~~~~~~~~~~~~

Seven-hundred-year-old Stockholm, capital of Sweden, rises picturesquely from fourteen islands. In the reign of famous Queen Kristina, this Viking village grew to a royal city where now the Nobel Prizes are conferred. A few tickets remain for our special tour to the Wasa.

But I'm not in the tourist mood this morning. I slept okay, but when I wake up it feels like a school-day. Peeling slowly out of the bunk, I see breakfast. Stavros never sleeps.

Taking a croissant for the road, I head down to the hospital to check on Shep. I'm fuzzy this morning. I was just getting used to a grandmother when a grandfather got slipped in on me.

It's a toy hospital, more like a doctor's office with a

few curtained beds. Only the nurse is on duty at this hour, lining up bottles of Compazine for the seasick. She lets me look in on Shep.

He's sleeping, or sleeping it off. The pajamas are the ones I found in his cabin, and they tend to humanize him. He looks a little more rested, through the stubble. I only mean to give him a glance, but I stand at the foot of the bed, searching him for clues, looking for links.

He's breathing easy, one arm thrown back, like any old guy sleeping in. In fact he looks pretty comfortable. I get a flash of anger at this guy who's got Connie so upset. Did he ever worry about anybody?

But I can't stop looking. I'm matching him up with his wedding picture. The next step is to match him up with me, but I don't get that far.

The curtains scrape back, and here's Connie's early-morning face. "I'm just . . ." She didn't expect to find me here. "I thought I better."

"Me too," I say.

She sees Shep from the corner of her eye. "I had to talk him over with Marty," she says, meaning the bandleader. So she's been busy this morning.

"It wasn't professional of me, you know. I don't do this kind of thing. I don't get people hired just because . . ." She half turns away. "They'll fill in with the lounge pianist, the one who takes requests in El Morocco. Then Shep can fly home to New York, whenever he's ready."

"Does he have a place in New York?"

"He's got an agent there." Her hand turns on the bar at the foot of the bed. "And that's it," she says. "That's where we let it go."

I nod.

"I was wrong about this. And I don't want you to get sentimental about something that never was."

"I won't," I say, answering for both Connie and me.

"Shep hasn't any use for your pity, or anybody's," she says, trying to clench this deal. "We never want pity."

When the nurse rustles on the far side of the curtains, Connie takes my hand, squeezing it more than she notices. "Come on. Let's get out of here. And don't come back down here, Drew. He'll get through it this time. They go on and on, you know. He'll be up again, up and thirsty. Let him go."

Out in the hall, I have to ask her. "Connie, if he'd been . . . in better shape, if it could have been the four of us together, would you have told him who Steph and I are?"

She shakes her head. "What for? He'd just think I was trying to pull something on him. I wouldn't have told him."

There's a bit of a swell this morning, and it's hard to walk a straight line. We veer toward walls as we go.

"Breakfast?"

"I'm not supposed to eat anything this morning,"

she says. "I'm not hungry. Let's take a turn up on the top deck."

But when we get up there, an aerobics class is filling the space, and unless my eyes deceive me, Helga's conducting it.

We're down on the Promenade Deck now, and Connie's had all the walk she wants. We settle into chairs across a small sidewalk-café table. It's nine o'clock, and she's exhausted. To cover, she watches the scenery going by. We're on the approach to Stockholm, with fancy villas rising out of fir forests.

"Your mother," she says, carefully.

Just that. And I've been waiting for it.

"You can see it wasn't a life for her. Look at Shep. Look at *me*." She pulls a thumb on herself. "I loved it all, but it wasn't what you'd want for your child."

She watches more villas.

"It was all right when she was little. I'd drag her around from pillar to post, like a rag doll. I'd take her on the road with me, and bed her down in a dresser drawer if there wasn't anything else."

She makes a little finger pattern on the tabletop. "Of course there were lean times when I didn't know where the next gig was coming from."

"People went home after the war," I say, "and television kept them home."

"That's right. When she started school, I'd have to keep taking her out of one and putting her in another. Finally, I sent her to boarding school. I didn't

137

know where the money was coming from. But, you know. You find it. She was about Stephanie's age then. I see now it wasn't the best time for us to . . . break up the act. Just when she came to the age of getting a little rebellious with me, I sent her away. I see now how she took that. You know how they are at that age."

"Do I ever," I say.

"I expect boys are just as bad," she says.

"No, girls are worse."

"If you're talking about Stephanie, don't sell that kid short."

But I'm beginning not to. "Is that why you and Mom don't have much of a relationship?"

She thinks that over and doesn't quite answer.

"If I could do it over, I'd find a way to keep her with me. I sent her off to get away from my kind of life. Then I didn't . . . follow where she went.

"I never even went to school myself, hardly, or ever knew anybody outside the business. And so she got to be like somebody out in an audience you can't quite reach with your song. Finally, she didn't even want to spend her vacations with me. She wanted to go stay with her friends. She wanted to be like other people."

She looks out the window again. "Anyway, you know how I am. I just pulled back and tended to my own business. I didn't want to butt in, and I . . . didn't want my feelings hurt. You take a lot of rejec-

138

tion in my business. You don't want to be turned down by your own child." She wipes the table clean of finger smudges.

"I'd never be any good at family life anyway. When your mother was a baby, I'd tip a hotel maid extra to come in and change her diapers. Wasn't that awful?"

"Worst thing I ever heard."

"Well, it wasn't that bad, but you know what I mean." She starts to reach across the table, but clasps her hands together instead. "She doesn't hate me, does she?" Her words ran together, and I almost didn't hear.

"Mom isn't that way. Maybe she's a little ashamed that life didn't work out perfect for her."

"You see?" Connie says. "That's another place where I went wrong. I dragged her around as a child, and it made her—what? Insecure. She wanted to be settled, and safe. Maybe she wanted it too much."

"Maybe," I say. "Maybe she's a little bit lonely, too, now that Dad's out of the picture and Steph and I are growing up. She's lonely. You could do something about that, Connie."

But the ship's horn gives out a tremendous blast. The waterway's widening into Stockholm Harbor, and we're coming into port. It's a long blast, and Connie's lips move, but they don't form a real word. She's on her feet, bustling, bristling, being Connie.

"You better take that guided tour they give," she

says. "They say it's interesting, and there's a ticket with your name on it down at the desk. You go on and do that. Stephanie and I are going off on our own today."

"Picking up where you left off?" I ask.

"What's that mean?"

"Are you starting with Steph where you left off with Mom?"

She turns, so I don't see her eyes.

"I might just do that, if I could. But you never repeat the same songs in the second set." Then she waves me away.

Like I say, I'm not in a tourist mood. But you can get so involved with adults, that you can't think. Then I'm on the tour bus, and they're all adults but me. I'm on the backseat, and it's nothing but gray heads ahead of me, like a flock of sheep. Now I know how a teacher feels—outnumbered.

We drive all over Stockholm, and my mind isn't on it. But then we stop to see the *Wasa*, which is this great old galleon ship, a man-of-war that sank three hundred years ago the day it was launched. This isn't the most encouraging sight for a bunch of people straight off a cruise ship, but it's interesting.

Solid oak, scientifically preserved, and carved all over, like a cathedral. They even brought up parts of its sails from the harbor bottom, and pewter utensils, and what was left of a sailor trapped by a loose can-

140

non. I'm nearly a tourist again by the time we get
back to the *Regal Voyager.*

And I'm barely back aboard before I'm surrounded
by—can it be?—Sandi and Jean. Either one of them
could surround me by herself, and they're leading
me away. Since I'm always the last to know, I'm the
last to know this is Costume Night, the biggest event
we get before Gala Night itself. Sandi and Jean con-
duct me down to a distant deck where big plans are
under way.

"Hey, I don't even have a costume," I say, not
hanging back.

"Och, not to worry," says Jean. "Holly says you
could wear nothing at all and go as Jacuzzi Man,
though you'd never win first prize."

"Not funny," I say, but Sandi's laughing her head
off. And so I'm swallowed up by the ship, surrounded
by centerfolds.

We work like crazy because it turns out to be more
than costumes, and it keeps involving more and
more people and supplies we have to go scrounging
for. It's like Homecoming. We grab some dinner off
the buffet and go on working.

The big moment's to be in the Adriatica Room
after the second seating for dinner. All the costumed
contenders are going to make a big promenade
across the stage for the rest of the passengers to see.
The band's going to play. They'll give out prizes, the
whole thing. And by show time, I'm really sweating.

There's a lot of electricity in the air. People and groups all over the ship are getting into weird costumes, hiding till the last minute. We're hard to hide. We end up putting ourselves together down on the crew's open deck, with the sea breeze blowing our props around.

Our entry is "Tivoli Trolley." It's a cardboard mock-up of the little Copenhagen roller-coaster ride that looks like a train. We've collected big cardboard cartons for the cars and painted them up. I'm the caboose. Holly's both engine and engineer, in a black leotard with a foil-covered saucer strapped to her forehead for a headlight, cardboard skirt like a cow-catcher—the works. The rest of the train's composed of cruise staff, along with Sandi—who's nobody's idea of a flatcar—and Helga with frosty hair and rhinestones, in a box that says REFRIGERATOR CAR. Jean's in a box upholstered with pillows. She's wearing a nightcap and carrying a candle because she's the sleeping car. Nobody asks what a sleeping car's doing on a freight train.

My caboose is a bright-red box hung on suspenders over my shoulders, with a lantern behind. We all have cardboard wheels. You have to use a little imagination, but we're a good train.

When the big moment approaches, we line up in order, to chug our way up through the ship. All the other contestants: the Arabs in ship's sheets, the Gypsies, the flappers, the punkers, one guy in a plastic curtain going as a shower stall, four old ladies as Beatles—that bunch are making their way to the Adriatica Room's backstage. But our train's different. We're going to come steaming in from the back of the room and work the audience before we highball it down onto the stage. We're going to make a big showing, and win.

From the minute we hit the rear of the Adriatica Room, it's show business. The crowd's already worked up. The waiters are getting the drinks around. Marty Wilhelm's Melodiers are updating with a medley from *The Sound of Music.*

But Tivoli Trolley holds back. We assemble up in the darkened room to watch the other contestants come onstage: a lady wearing bananas and doing a dance, a small squadron of Joan Riverses, a wimpy guy with a Tom Selleck mask, four old gents in hula skirts, a mature lady with a headband and a toy machine gun as Rambo, the sheet Arabs.

We wait for the right moment. Holly blows a whistle; we form up and roll out. Somebody's already lit my lantern. We snake along through the tiers of tables, and our arms are pumping like pistons. A waiter gets in the way but sees Holly's cowcatcher, and moves. The spotlight finds us. Anywhere else but on a ship, this could be seriously embarrassing. Here, it's great.

We're still working the rows, getting down nearer the stage, and we've stopped the show. The cruise director's leading the applause. The Rambo lady wants to waste us.

I spot the Krebses at ringside, and Steph and Connie sitting with them. Even the audience wears masks, but you can spot them. Connie's is silver paper with fake jewels, standing up like a crown. She's smiling, clapping.

Steph in a purple mask is next to her, slumped. I just catch a glimpse, but she's close to Connie, practically in her lap. I happen to notice Melanie on the aisle in one of her upscale outfits and a white mask with feathers. They're all giving us a big hand.

The train swerves onto the stage past them, and the caboose follows. I reach over the side of my red box for Melanie's hand, and she draws back. But we make contact. She's on her feet, with her fingers over her face being, like, so embarrassed she could die.

There's just room for her in my caboose if she dips under and comes up beside me. She does, and we catch up with the rest of the train, a four-legged caboose bringing up the rear. We win first prize, a bottle of champagne which the cruise director has already popped the cork on, spraying us all.

The Melodiers break into "Chattanooga Choo-Choo," and Melanie, plastered beside me, sighs. "This is like . . . so . . . seriously . . . neat." And from the front of the train, the engine looks back, flashes on us with her headlight, and gives me one of her sly looks.

144

Everybody stays up for the block-long midnight buffet in the Magellan Room. The centerpiece is a hollow ice sculpture of the *Regal Voyager* with candles inside. It's floating on a Jell-O lake surrounded by pineapple forests and layer cakes shaped like snowcapped mountains. You eat on your feet, up against masked people. Out the portholes it's either gray evening or dawn at sea because this is practically the shortest night of the year.

Or the longest. I'm dragging my tail on the way to the cabin, and when I get down here, I can only crash on the edge of my bed. I can't even get around to taking off my railroader's cap, or wonder where I got it. We seem to do a lot of living on this ship. I try to remember life before this cruise, but it's hazy. I was a kid in school somewhere. I had this friend named what's-his-name.

Somebody knocks on my door. Stavros, no doubt, wondering if I'm hungry.

It's Steph. She's knocked. Now she's inside, leaning back against the closed door. I wonder if she's growing, but it's the two-inch silver shoes, with white pants a lot like Melanie's and a sweater with silver threads in it. There's something wrong with her face. Blurry purple lines arch over both her cheeks. She's fiddling with her purple eye mask, twisting the elastic string.

"What's wrong with your face? You look like a badger."

She throws her mask on the floor.

"You've been crying. Why?"

"That's a lie," she says. "It's sweat."

Whatever. But she's been crying.

"Or spray," she says. "Connie went to bed before the buffet, and I went up on deck, to be alone."

"But now you're here."

"Now I'm here."

"You ought to get some sleep. You're zonked."

"I could sleep a month," she says. "If we ever get home, I will. Move over."

She drops down on the drop-down bed beside me. She doesn't flop. Her shoes are making her more graceful, or something. When she crosses her legs, one small foot in a shoe swings in the air. She looks like a scaled-down woman: Connie, in fact. When she starts working her hand over her pursed mouth, it's total Connie, down to the fingernails.

She picks up the mask and starts twisting it into shapes, making a mess of it. Then she sniffs loud. Suddenly it's the old Steph again because she elbows me hard with a quick jab to the ribs. No warning, and it hurts.

"You are so dumb, you don't know anything," she says, but softly. "And take off that dumb cap. You look like a farmer."

"Steph. What?"

"Nothing."

"Steph?"

"It's Connie, and I don't see how you can be so d—"

"What about her?"

"For one thing, she treats me like I'm brain dead. Like I'm a . . . sixth grader or something." Steph shudders. "And for another—"

Her voice breaks. She leans over on me, butting her head against me till I put my arm around her. I can feel the first sob working up through her. She's crying now, without a sound, and my shirt's damp. This isn't the old Steph staging a tantrum. She's fought these tears back, and they've won. I fit my chin over her head, and hold her.

When she stops, she's on her feet, pretending she isn't half blind. She sinks onto the chair, pulling herself together. Why do I have the feeling she's just cried away the last of the old Steph?

"You want to wait till morning to—"

"It is morning, if we had portholes," she says. "It never really gets dark in these places. How do people rest?"

A sob comes up dry in her, and she swallows hard. "Connie's sick. She's really sick, and I don't mean seasick, which she never is."

She's smoothed out the bandana over her knees, and folded it across in a triangle.

147

"She had a mastectomy in the spring. You know what that is?"

". . . Yeah."

"It's having her breast removed. We dress together in that stupid cabin, and she showed me. She has special bras built up on one side. She's . . . smooth. One side of her is. And her arm on that side is weak. Every time she lifts it up, it hurts her. She moans when nobody's around but me. She moans when she turns over in her sleep."

I picture Steph lying in their cabin, awake. Hearing.

"And she doesn't wear those wigs because she wants to. Or those turban things. She had chemotherapy, and her hair fell out. It's growing back, but not much yet, not enough to cover her head. She hates those wigs, right?"

"Right."

"Then this morning—yesterday, Connie took me with her in—where?"

"Stockholm."

"We went to the Karolinska Institute there. It's a research place for cancer. She'd gone there first when the ship stopped in Stockholm on the other cruise. They had her records from home, and they gave her another test. This time she went back for the results."

". . . What were the results?"

"Do I know?" Steph's red eyes snap. "I'm not supposed to know anything. I was out in that waiting room for a hundred years, and finally she comes out . . . smiling and everything. And she just goes, 'Looks like I've got a clean bill of health. Let's go eat smorgasbord someplace.' "

Steph whips around and slams her fist down on the table. "How dumb am I supposed to be all of a sudden? We learned about this in school, in Health. She'd had another test at that Karolinska place, and they gave her bad news."

"You don't know that," I say, but I say it carefully.

"I bet she's found a lump on her other breast. And I bet they tested her, and this time when she went back to find out, they told her they couldn't do . . . anything. They told her the cancer had spread, and it's too late."

"You mean if they'd kept her there and operated, it would have been better? If they'd taken off her other breast, it would have been a—good thing?"

Steph nods.

"That's probably not it," I say. "She probably just went in for a routine exam. You have to do that, after an operation."

It sounds right when I say it, but Steph's not buying. "If it had been routine, Connie would have said so, up front. I saw her face when she walked in the door of that place. I know Connie."

Steph's taking short, quick breaths, with sobs behind. "If she'd just told me, like she told me about the wigs and the bra. If she'd just tell me, I could handle it. But what am I supposed to do with this?"

She puts out her hands. She's been getting older, just lately. Why can't she get a little credit for it?

"Connie didn't tell me anything at all," I say.

The old Steph would have looked smug. This one just says, "You know now."

It's quiet then, so I say, "She's proud."

"And stubborn," Steph says. "She's the stubbornest person I ever knew, right?"

". . . Right. One of them." I pull off my cap, and Steph's at the door, but she turns around.

"Back in the spring when she had her operation, I bet she knew. She figured she wasn't going to be— around much longer. That's why we're here."

And maybe that's why she went looking for Shep. Maybe she just wanted us to be together, once in her life. Maybe she couldn't risk Mom, but she wanted the rest of us here—family. Maybe she just wanted to be able to look around that dinner table in the Magellan Room, and see us.

"It's not fair," Steph says, her oldest saying, dredged up. "We just got here, and she's . . . going. If we hadn't ever known her, we wouldn't miss her. She should have left us alone."

"No, she shouldn't. I wouldn't have wanted to miss her."

Steph's hand is behind her back, closed over the door handle. She's thinking about going, and staying.

She's trying not to cry, but it doesn't matter now. "Me either," she says, and her voice falls apart.

I wouldn't mind if she went now and left me alone. I'd like to work up some denial about this whole deal. If I tried, I might make myself believe Steph's wrong. But I'm sure she's not. This is as sure as I've ever been about anything.

"Come on back. Sit down."

She's stumbling back and flopping down beside me. She sniffs again and digs one of her silver heels into my carpet.

"I ought to come right out and ask her," she says, mumbling. "I ought to just wake her up and say, 'Do you have another lump? Did they tell you it's, you know, malignant?' I would, too, except she's sleeping like a log. You can practically hear her from here. She sneaks catnaps during the day too. Tomorrow she has to rehearse all day for that dumb Gala Night coming up. Otherwise, I'd go in there right now, and make her talk. . . ."

I let Steph run down, and we sit there awhile. Then she says, "You could talk to her, Drew."

She's sketching little invisible finger patterns on her knee.

"Why me?" I say, one of my older sayings.

"Because we can't just walk away from her at the end of this cruise, without any words. We can't let her walk away from us. Forget that." Steph's almost lean-

151

ing on me. I can feel the warmth of her all down my side. "Anyway, you're the oldest."

Wait a minute. "How come I'm just now getting credit for being older, all of a sudden?"

"You are. You're in high school. I'm just a . . . kid." She tucks her feet away so you can't see her high heels.

"Do you want me to call Mom?" I could. You can call from the ship, and, boy, do I want to. It's even fair, isn't it? She ought to be told. I want to dump this whole thing right in Mom's lap—no, not dump, but—

"I thought about calling her," Steph says. "I went all the way up to the radio room. But I didn't call."

"Why not?"

"Do I know? I just didn't. For one thing I thought about her being there alone, when the phone rang."

"You never worried about Mom being alone before."

She digs me, but lightly. "I think maybe Mom knows anyway," she says. "Maybe that's one reason Connie didn't invite her along—because she knew. Maybe Connie didn't want this to be . . . that kind of trip."

"Do you think Connie told her?"

"Maybe she didn't have to. Sometimes adults know things. You better think of something else, Drew."

"I think we're going to have to play it Connie's way."

That's not going to satisfy Steph, and I'm not sure

it's going to satisfy me. What I'd like to do is cry, and somehow this isn't the time.

My elbow's wedged between my side and Steph, but I put my hand out. She notices, and puts her hand in mine. Hers is half the size of mine except for the fingernails. I don't think we've ever done this before.

Finally when she goes, she goes quietly. She doesn't want to wake Connie.

Chapter 11

We have a day at sea between Stockholm and—where? Possibly Oslo. I was up till four or five, maybe later, so I miss the first two meals of the day. But when I get going, I head up to a deck chair in that quiet area between the funnels on top deck.

I want some sun on my anxieties, so I'm down to my Speedos again. The ship's pitching around too much for the tennis players, and the other sun worshipers are all back down on the fantail around the outdoor pool.

The day's weirdly normal. Steph's gone looking for Melanie, and Connie's down in the Adriatica Room, rehearsing the new piano player, easing him into the band. Gala Night's coming up, and a lot of momentum is building for that. People are really ready to hear Connie sing again. I'm in no hurry. It'll be the last night out, and I'm not ready for last nights.

154

It's a Scandinavian summer seascape up here. I'm in a windbreak, and the sound of the flags snapping in the breeze is a tranquilizer. From the corner of one drooping eyelid I see how the forward funnel takes a white bite out of the blue sky. My pores are hermetically sealed with coconut oil quick-tanner, and I'm ready to drop into my coma. The pitch this high in the ship rocks my cradle.

I'm halfway to dreamland. It's that moment before real sleep when three naked female seniors always come tripping across my landscape. But suddenly I'm not so asleep again. I'm about half out, sun dazed, when Connie's here, between me and the sun.

Not really. Actually she's down in the Adriatica Room in a tight turban, ordering the band around. But she's up here, too, real enough to claim my attention. She's shaking her head, and she means it. She's just this black silhouette against the sun, but it glints off the points of her glasses frames.

And *No*, she's telling me, *No*, and what does it mean? *No, I'm not dying?* Or *No, we're not going to talk about it.*

Which? I know what I want to believe, though it's a little late for that. But she won't say any more. I can see through her now: first the railing behind her and the circle of a life preserver. Then the open sea glints where her glasses had been.

But still I don't get any privacy. My eyes are shut now, though I can see through the red blood-vessels of my lids. Shep's here, wearing his sauna towel. The blood vessels in my eyelids become the blue veins in his legs. He's a stooped shape turned away from the sun because he's not much of a day person. With a good grip on his towel.

If he gives me a sign, a little wave good-bye, I'll be fine. If we can manage a moment here of recognizing each other before he goes, then at least that part will be a neat wrap-up.

But he's on his way already, and I can see right through him. No wave. He doesn't even call me a law firm. People go when they have to, not when it suits you.

If I'm not asleep, I wish I were. The towel's still here. Steph's wearing it, a ghost of the old Steph clutching a Clarence Hotel towel around her training bra and flowered bikini pants. And so we're all the way back to the beginning of this trip. Steph's doing a barefoot war dance and silently screaming, *Do something.*

That about calls the roll. Except that Mom's standing over by the rail, too alone. And I can't make out what she knows, or whether she knows. She's looking out to sea, and what's she doing in her tweed go-to-work suit on a cruise?

The ship's really pitching now. The sun seems to flame out, and at last I rock into deep space.

Then something happens to time. I'm on my stomach in the deck chair, so I could be getting too much sun on my back. I'm looking through plastic webbing down at the fake grass on the deck.

Something's gone wrong with the world. I know not to raise my head, but I can look out to sea through the bars on the railing. Even the horizon is acting up. And the ship's doing some terrible trick. It rises up on the crest of the wave, hangs there, and then drops down. It does it again. It keeps doing it. My body doesn't want to hang on the crest of a wave and then drop down. Something's rising in me. It starts low and builds.

With a superb act of will, I'm up and ready to make a run for the rail. But my foot goes through the webbing, and I'm wearing my deck chair. I vomit all over my bottle of quick-tanner. My knees buckle. I'm crawling across the fake grass, and we're the same color. Uphill, then downhill. Uphill, then . . .

I come to, more or less, down in my cabin where it's eternal night. I was never completely blitzed. I seem to remember deckhands lifting me off the deck and carrying me down through the slanting ship. Now I'm back on my bunk, in bed with a large basin which I'm hugging.

I seem to have a touch of seasickness, and it appears to be fatal. Even my cabin has lost its senses. Things chase each other around on the table. The hangers in my closet are playing the "Anvil Chorus." I'm ready to make a deal here. I'll give up girls for the

157

rest of my natural life if somebody will just turn off the surf machine.

"Truly?"

I must have said that last line out loud. Somebody's sitting next to my bunk. A deathwatch? I can't turn my head. I can't move my lips from the rim of my basin, where they belong. But I know who's sitting there. Even that one word was in an English accent. In only my Speedos I probably seem to be stark naked under this blanket, and I suppose it figures.

"Holly?" I say, hollow because my basin echoes.

"Yes, darling."

"Is this the end?"

"Well, let's say your dancing days are over, but then they never began, did they?"

"How is everybody else?"

"Oh, fighting fit. We're taking you in turns. We're on tonight. You remember the fabulous French foursome? We're backing up the comedian for the dinner show, and, heavens, how he needs it. I'm sorry to tell you that you slept through Helga."

I groan, but not for Helga.

"And Steph? How's she doing?"

"This afternoon I noticed that she and Melanie were being removed from the slot machines in El Morocco for being underage. She looked a little cross, but otherwise quite on the top of her form."

"And Connie?"

158

"She broke up the rehearsal early to sit with you first. She emptied your basin twice."

Twice? "Why can't I even remember that?"

"I shouldn't think you'd care to."

"Where's Connie now?"

"Still at dinner, I imagine. She said she could eat a horse."

That does it. Something starts up from the pit of my stomach like an express train. It *is* the pit of my stomach. I've cleared out the contents, and so now here comes the lining. I turn into a tortured pretzel and heave dry. The pain's unbelievable, like knives. And there's no relief in sight. I could keep this up possibly till Oslo.

"Poor poppit," Holly murmurs. She lays a cool hand on my fiery bare shoulder. If I weren't terminal with seasickness, I'd be writhing with sunburn. If I live, I'll peel. I'm having a wonderful time on this cruise. A sudden attack of sadness makes my eyes water, and now they tear. I'd sob, but it would hurt. "Holly, you mean I'm the only one sick?"

"I expect there are others. There were some empty chairs in the dining room."

"Don't mention dining room. Or the f-word. You know, food."

"No, darling. I lost my head."

"You're on tonight?" I say.

"Yes, backing up the comedian. A few high kicks

159

and that medley from *Sound of Music.* Somehow, I don't think we'll need anything for an encore."

"How can you, with the ship doing . . . this?"

"We've been at it for ages. My first time out, I fell through the bass drum, but you learn balance. We could do the whole show at a forty-five-degree angle. We'd have been the last ones off the *Lusitania*."

My stomach lurches, but I may be past the worst.

"Holly, if I could turn over, would I see you in your —costume?"

"Yes, Drew. Just a scatter of spangles and an egret feather. Hardly enough to keep the chill off."

I make the sacrifice. My lips leave the basin, and I turn my racked body over on my burning shoulders for a good look at Holly. She's sitting here in a flannel wrapper buttoned to the throat. Her hair's tied up in a towel that reads OLYMPIC HOTEL, ATHENS. She doesn't have her makeup on. Her eyes are greener without it.

I sigh. "As Steph used to say, I'm so betrayed I can't believe it."

"You couldn't remain there forever, surrounding your basin," Holly says.

"This basin is my best friend." I give it another hug.

Holly looks every bit as good completely wrapped. I notice this, so I may be on the road to recovery, a small first step. "But how come I'm so sick? I had my sea legs."

"Ummm," she says, "but it strikes people in different ways, and some not at all. And there are always those who are violently sick while we're still tied up at the dock." Holly looks slightly aside. "And maybe you were ready to be sick. Maybe you were already upset."

I give that some thought. It's true, being this sick conveniently takes your mind off everything else. We're quiet for a while, except for the wavering walls that crackle and groan.

"You know about Connie?"

When she looks down, there's only a triangle of brilliant red hair showing beneath her Olympic towel.

"Not really. I only know she's a very independent woman who goes it alone. And suddenly she reaches out a long way for her grandchildren, and their grandfather. It would make you wonder, if you were watching."

I lie there, my eyes stinging. The closet hangers are playing softer. "Tell me some more, about Connie."

Holly folds the tails of her wrapper over her knees.

"She has a gift. She can make an audience of people just her age be young again, and in love with each other. She can take them back in ways she can't go back herself. It's what she does best—none better. I expect she wanted you to see that."

Holly gets quiet, and so I say, "You're really smart."

"Not so smart. Not clever. But I live in a world of

161

strangers, and it sharpens your eye." She thinks a moment and remembers something else, a detail. "And the wigs. Connie would dye her hair, but she wouldn't wear wigs unless she had to."

I guess I needed to hear all this, from someone else, from Holly. "I say you're smart."

"Dancers aren't dumb. That's only a cliché." Something prim happens to her mouth, and she adds, "Except for Sandi."

But I'm not out of the woods yet. I drift through time, in and out of awareness. At one point Stavros leaves a pot of tea, but I keep my distance. The Greek doctor makes a house call and gives me a shot. I remember him saying, *"Kali nikhta,"* so it must have been night because that means "Good night." People come and go. Sometime after the shot I'm checked out by a big pair of violet bifocals bending over me, but then they're gone again. Steph drops by. Who else would give a dying man a sharp jab to the rib cage?

Chapter *12*

Oslo, the "Countryside Capital" of Norway, opens its welcoming arms at the top of its own fjord. It's the oldest capital (1050 A.D.) of Scandinavia's new-est country, for Norway won its independence from our old friends, the Swedes and Danes, only in 1905. Enjoy your day by selecting one of our personally conducted tours of this carefree, compact urban environment.

This news has been slipped under my door. I've been out of bed a couple of times and down on all fours, exploring my floor and dragging my basin. I've put on a pair of chinos and socks, but I don't need a shirt over my lobster shoulders.

I sit on the floor and read up on Oslo, but it's going to have to get along without me. Anyway, we're at sea, believe me. My Swatch says it's quarter past seven, which could mean anything. The door behind me flies open and slams my back, leaving a line on my sunburn I'll remember for a long time. Someone enters, Reebok first.

"What do you think you're doing on the floor? Move over. I want in." But Steph's already in, and peering down at my reading matter. "Forget Oslo. We've done that. It was neat. They had a big ski jump, and Melanie and I shopped."

"Did you just get back?"

Steph stares. "What is this, *Twilight Zone*? Oslo was *yesterday*. We're at *sea*." My hangers jingle on cue. "Tomorrow's our last day."

Tomorrow being our last day seems to slow her down. "How do you feel?"

"Ever hear of Shake 'n Bake?"

"You haven't eaten anything in days. Stavros is going out of his skull. Aren't you hungry? I could do with about a pound of trail mix."

I make a grab for my basin just in case, but I seem to be okay. I could probably stand up if I had a really good reason. And maybe I do, because Steph's throwing my closet door open. I catch a glimpse of myself as the mirror on the door swings my way. Under my flaming sunburn I'm dull green. I look like old Christmas wrap.

"You've got to get your act together," she says.

"For one thing, Stavros wants your sheets. He's supposed to change them every day."

"You know when we get home, Steph, we're not going to get this kind of service."

"Forget home," she says, flipping through my small tie collection. "You've got to be up tonight and dressed." She shifts past my white dinner jacket on the way to my blue blazer. "I hope you've got a clean shirt."

"Steph, I'm down a couple of days and you turn into Hitler. What's happening?"

"Nothing," she says, snappy. "Especially in this hole. Get up. People are worried about you."

I get up, but my chinos don't. I've lost another inch around the waist. I'm down to a twenty-seven.

"Do you know how bad this place smells?" Steph leans into my bathroom and turns on the shower. "Wash all over."

"I'm not having dinner. Forget that."

"Who cares? But you've got to be up in the 'A' suite on Mykonos Deck by nine-thirty."

"Mykonos? That's the top deck. I don't go up there anymore."

"You'll go tonight. For one thing, Holly's going to be up there."

"What's going on? Will Connie be there?"

Steph makes the little family tick sound in her throat. "Connie too."

She stands, squinty eyed, being incredibly bossy.

Her sweatshirt reads NORGE, which might mean Norway. Clouds of steam puff out of the bathroom. "I mean it, Drew. You've been sick long enough. I think you're . . . disorientated. I think you threw up your brains."

That's a real possibility. I climb up from the floor in stages. My microwaved skin strains and pops. My stomach's a black hole in space. "Steph, my pants are around my knees. Do you want to be here when I take off my shorts?"

She goes.

I'm showered and dressed, though it took me the full two hours. Twenty minutes alone to ease on a shirt, another half hour for the tie. I've had to reinvent familiar routines. Stavros tied my shoes.

Before I navigate the Coral Deck hallway, I stop across the hall to see if anybody's home at Connie and Steph's. Their cabin's a bomb site, the recent scene of a dressing orgy. The floor's lumpy with shoes, and the hair dryer's still plugged in. The smell of Connie's favorite perfume hangs in the air—Tabu. Otherwise it's empty.

We've still got some side-to-side motion, but going down the hall, I roll with the punches. I take the elevator, and it stops on every deck. I'd forgotten how many people are on this ship. They're in and out of the elevator, coming and going. It's the rush hour between the second seating and the dinner show. On the Adriatica level a billboard announces Milo the

Magnificent and his rabbit, Stu, backed up by the baritone and Marty Wilhelm's Melodiers. Life goes on.

Up on Mykonos Deck it's quieter, though a few parties are going on in suites. I detour out on the open deck, the scene of my recent disaster-at-sea. It's full daylight with an evening feel. We're still off the Land of the Midnight Sun. I test myself with a quick look at the ocean. A few whitecaps out there, but nothing I can't manage. The collapsed balloon of my stomach doesn't even lurch.

I head forward to the "A" suite. It seems to take up the whole front of the ship, with a double door at the end of the hall. I wonder what I'm doing here, give my tie a final yank, and knock.

The doors open, and there's nothing but whiskers and gold braid. It's the captain in his dress whites, the Captain of the Ship. I've only seen him at boat drill and up on the bridge. He's bigger in real life, incredibly impressive, and Greek.

"Meester Drew Wingate?"

I barely catch my name. He gestures me inside with an enormous hand, sort of a command. Suite "A" is the captain's own quarters. The room's huge and there must be more. You could house fifty Coral Deck–type people in here. Oversized furniture, a lot of art on the walls, and in the distance a long table with flowers and candles.

A woman's posed at the far end in a long red gown

that sweeps off one shoulder and down to the floor. A small woman, but she looms large. Her hair's black, glossy in the candlelight, and her eyebrows are high arches. Her fingernails are endless, redder than her gown. Connie.

She comes forward, her arms out a little stagy, but there's something private in her face, something for me. It's Connie-the-famous-singer in all her war paint and ankle-strap shoes with the platform soles to give her height. But it also happens to be my grandmother. It's one of those dreams where nothing fits, and everything works.

She always puts her lips on with a little brush, and tonight she's been extra accurate. Her head's at a familiar angle, and she's doing without her glasses. The captain stands back, smiling behind his whiskers.

Now Connie's close, looking up at me. She's been trailing a long silk scarf, and in that hand is an envelope. She hands it over. It's a radio message, my first. I open it and read:

> To Drew:
> Special love, especially today.
> Mom

Still, I don't know.

"I wish I'd been there the other fifteen times," Connie says. "I'm glad I'm here now."

168

Then it hits me. Like thunder. Today is my sixteenth birthday.

I've been waiting to be sixteen forever. This is the big time. Looking forward to this is what got me through junior high. This is the day I was going to get my driver's license and start bagging babes. I've been on hold for this day since birth, and I nearly slept through it. Why am I always the last to know? But it's still daylight through the curtained windows. I haven't missed it.

"I didn't know what to give you," Connie says, "so I give you a party."

I take her hands. But the room's gone fuzzy, and my tongue's dead meat. Steph's right. I threw up my brains. But I've got to rise to this. I'm not fifteen anymore, you know.

"I don't need a party. You're enough."

We have that moment before the room explodes. Doors fly open, and waiters barge in, bearing silver trays. A chandelier blazes, and it's full of balloons. Champagne corks detonate on the ceiling. People appear from everywhere, from behind chairs, curtains. The Lady-of-Spain accordionist leaps out from nowhere and splits the air with "Happy Birthday" to a beat all his own.

Everybody's here: Steph and Melanie in matching glitter tops and the Krebses and a bunch more of Connie's groupies. Milo the Magnificent's popped in just before his show, and Stu pops out of his hat. Nico

169

from the Magellan Room is one of the waiters. And Holly and Jean and Helga and Sandi, all in high gloves and low formals, like prom night in heaven. And Holly has a special little smile for me because I've been seventeen up till now.

When the cake comes in, it's four tiers tall supported by white-sugar Greek columns and 16 in tall chocolate numbers surrounded by frosting roses. It arrives on a silver trolley. I'm even a little hungry, and I better be because grinning Stavros is manning the trolley.

And everybody's singing. High up above this ocean in Europe or somewhere, everybody's singing, and I'm sixteen.

I wake up in stages late the next afternoon, almost evening. It looks like I've brought the party back down to Coral Deck. Balloons bob on my ceiling, and there's tickertape everywhere, the kind people throw on sailing day. I got a lot of joke presents, souvenirs people picked up at ports: a complete tribe of carved Scandinavian trolls, a box of Russian chocolates with Lenin on the lid, several national flags, and a really good present from the captain: a silver bowl with the *Regal Voyager* etched on it—a VIP-type gift. Stu gave me a candy carrot.

There's still a pint of champagne and a slab of cake in me, which has left my stomach speechless. Stavros has brought my lunch: an Alka-Seltzer.

We're still at sea, the North Sea again, and none too smooth. My mirrored closet door is swinging back and forth, and I see me in passing. I've lost some weight in the neck, and my eyes are pretty far back in my head. But some of my sunburn has gone tan, and I ought to have a couple of days before real peeling. Better yet, my hair's bleaching out in front. What with the neck and the red beak and the hair standing up, I look like a surprised chicken, but I'm on the road to recovery.

And sixteen. And somewhere around the world, so is Bates Morthland. Good old Bates. It occurs to me that with the difference in time, I turned sixteen seven hours ahead of him. This may not make up for the Jeep Wrangler Sahara that's bound to come with his driver's license, but it gets me out of bed.

Stavros has lined up my shoes, and there's confetti in one of them. Dimly I remember we moved the party down to the disco at one point. Next to my shoes is a long tube of paper, tied with a ribbon, like a big diploma.

Still dim, I remember this is my present from Holly, Helga, Jean, and Sandi, and I'm not to open it until I get to my room. But I haven't gotten around to it. The bow is still as perky as Sandi.

As it unrolls, I see it's a poster . . . a blown-up photograph, full color, of me in a blue blazer surrounded by flesh tones. Five people around a table in Helsinki—me being lunched by four practically naked beauties in a European capital. It's fantastic, and it's proof, and it's the size of my locker door.

Getting away from me, it rerolls itself. And suddenly I'm bolt awake and panicked. Time's slipping away, too fast. Already I'm surrounded by souvenirs, and I don't want this to be over, ever. I start stumbling around on my shoes. Today's the last day, and tonight's . . .

. . . Gala Night. I'm in my white dinner jacket, and Steph's in her blue formal. She's been to the ship's hairdresser for a mature styling and cut: feathery, high-school. She's wearing an orchid. I got it for her.

We're at ringside in the Adriatica Room at a table for three, Steph, Connie, and I. Dinner took two hours. They pulled out all the stops in the Magellan Room. This is the last night, the night we hand over our tips to the waiters, and they shower us with extras. The meal had ten courses, and everything was served either on ice or in flames. And already people were starting to say good-bye.

There's only one show tonight, so everybody's here, mostly standing, sitting on the steps, jammed in. The Melodiers are doing loud medleys, one after another: *Oklahoma! South Pacific, My Fair Lady.* Nobody's dancing. Nobody can get to the dance floor. The Adriatica Room flickers with jewels, and elec-

172

tricity. There's no room to breathe in here, so it's all got to go like clockwork.

The cruise director comes on to tell us what a great time we've had on this trip, and then he brings on each entertainer in turn. The baritone gives us "Some Enchanted Evening," and we bring him back for "The Best of Times Is Now," which has been the theme song for the whole cruise. Stu and Milo do a couple of tricks, and the crowd loves it all. They're even pretty tolerant of the comedian and give him some charity chuckles. The accordionist knows to give them "Lady of Spain" again.

It's a generous audience, but they're waiting for Connie. I don't think they see her down here at the table with us. She's sitting quiet behind her darkest glasses, being ready. She's in the dugout, and she's coming up to bat. And it's late in the game.

The lights begin to move from white through blue and purple to pink. We're getting back to the 1940s, peeling away the years. While we're distracted by the lighting, Holly, Helga, Jean, and Sandi appear in the background, in long-ago dresses. They begin to sing, close harmony, and it's a number called "Bei Mir Bist Du Schoen." It's 1945, and they're a group called the Andrews Sisters: Patti, LaVerne, Maxine, and a spare.

They're better dancers than singers, but it's okay. The audience begins to send something back. People are craning their necks, looking for Connie.

The lights dim and come up on the captain in his whiskers and gold braid. Nobody expects him here, and he's crossing in front of the Andrews Sisters, coming downstage. Then he's bowing over our table, and Connie rises, to the occasion.

As he starts to lead her onto the stage, she turns back, drops her glasses on the table, and says to Steph and me, "Watch this. I'm going to knock their hats in the creek."

The captain leaves her at center stage. In a room full of diamonds, she's standing alone in a plain black dress, black as her hair and her platformless shoes. No long scarf to do business with, and she's a shade paler than she was on the first night. Under the lights she always grows taller, but not so much tonight.

She lets them see her almost as she really is, to quiet them. Then she speaks. "I'll have to do it anyhow, so let's get it out of the way."

She goes into "Swingtime Down in Dixie," almost ahead of the band. The years drop off her, off everybody. She begins to work the stage, and she's twenty-five years old again, tops. Behind her the Andrews Sisters move and mime, snap their fingers. They back her up and keep out of her way.

By the time her shoes begin to blur, we've got our whole lives ahead of us. When she ends, her feet are far apart, and her hands are high, and the first of the flowers start falling around her.

She gives us the show we've been waiting for. She

talks us out of ourselves and into her hands: about how she first sang "Smoke Rings" in front of the Casa Loma Orchestra. How she stole "Cow Cow Boogie" from Ella Mae Morse. When she sings Ted Weems's "Heartaches," she touches her heart, her breast. She weaves her spell, and we're there in her net.

"I've Got My Love to Keep Me Warm," she says, and then sings it. She does extra sets, and doesn't make us beg. She's not even sweating, and I know why. This is her last performance, ever. Tonight she's going to do it all and be her best. Not a song short, not a note. I can't look at her for a moment. I look down at the table and see Steph's hands. Chubby wrists and hands clenched hard, white at the knuckles, because she knows too.

Connie's singing another song now, and toward the end of the refrain, she sends a signal back to the band as she moves downstage. The spot follows her till it falls across our table. Her hand's out for me, and she's leading me onto the floor. She turns, and I tower over her. The overhead lights are broiling. The audience watches, wordless, until we begin to dance.

It's ridiculous. She only comes up to the third button on my shirt. I feel the little bones in her back, and how light she moves. I won't step on her foot. She won't let it happen. We can do no wrong tonight. The audience sighs to see Connie dancing with her grandson, on the last night out. And I remember the

175

song she's just sung. It's "I'll Get By," and maybe it's a message.

I'm back at the table, numb and shaky, sweating through my shirt. But there are still a couple songs to go. The show's run over an hour, but nobody notices. I don't know what I'm noticing, except that the piano player's a fill-in. And somehow I know that Shep flew home from Oslo.

"We've been down memory lane," Connie's telling us. "We've been down in Dixie and down Mexico way. We've gone all the way back, and yet we're still here. We're the lucky ones because the best of times is now."

She sings it then, and when her eyes sweep over Steph and me, she isn't counting the house. She adds this modern song to her antique ones, and it fits. It's her final blending.

Then she's turning to go. She's been so generous we can't believe she'd pull this. As she starts off, her hand just brushes the sweep of the white grand piano, and she pats the substitute player on the shoulder. And so yes, Shep's gone, but the beat goes on.

But then she turns back to the roaring, stamping crowd. Her eyes are surprised, each lash applied separately. And she goes into it: "Do Nothing Till You Hear from Me."

It's her big one, the biggest, and she pours it over us like honey. She purrs, and plays with it, shifting tempo until it's almost another song. She lets it run long, longer than a song. But that's okay. She's entitled. Then she begins to wrap it up and hand it to us. It's like the first song you ever heard, from the first singer. It'd be great if Mr. Morthland was here. You don't get this on acetate. This is just for now, here.

She makes it her finish, easing out of it, and the lights go dark. We can stand up and applaud all night. We can take the place apart. But the show's over.

Tomorrow we'll wake up at the dock in England and fly home from Heathrow. And Connie flies back to Florida. We have to leave our luggage out in the hall tonight, and let's assume Steph will remember not to pack everything.

Time's running out, the way time does. All through her show tonight, Connie's been saying good-bye, her way. This is how she wants us to remember her, and tell Mom.

What Steph and I want is for Connie to change her plans and come home with us, for a visit—to stay, for as long as she can. But she's stubborn. She's definitely one of the stubbornest people I ever knew. And proud.

So I've got a big job tomorrow, my biggest to date. Tomorrow I have to be something more than sixteen —and silent. I'm going to have to stand there in an airport with my arm around Steph. And we're going to have to let Connie walk away. She'll help. She won't look back.

About the Author

One of the most popular and highly acclaimed authors of young adult fiction, Richard Peck writes books for teenaged readers urging them to act independently of their peers. His books, he says, are to "encourage young people not to sit up in the bleachers, cheering a team they never made." His themes explore friendship in place of peer-group cloning, and celebrate young individuals looking for their own strengths "while everybody else is looking for a leader." Through comedy, mystery, romance, and realism, Mr. Peck pursues his theme of young readers looking for themselves.

Richard Peck attended Fxeter University in England and holds degrees from DePauw University and Southern Illinois University. His novels for young adults include *Secrets of the Shopping Mall Remembering the Good Times, Close Enough to Touch,* and *Blossom Culp and the Sleep of Death.* Three of his novels have been filmed for television. His most recent book for Delacorte Press is *Princess Ashley.*

Richard Peck lives in New York City.